VACANT

S. Graham

To Donna,

Happy Reading!

S. [signature]

This book is inspired by true events, and includes fictional work. Some of the names, characters, businesses, places, events and incidents in this book may be the product of the author's imagination or used in a fictitious manner. Any resemblance to actual persons, living or dead, or actual events may be purely coincidental.

For my family.

CONTENTS

CHAPTER 1

Each October, thousands of haunted houses open up all across the country. Thrill-seekers look for the heart-pumping jump scare, letting out the screams of pure terror. Actors posing as zombies, dolls, clowns, ghosts, and children all wanting one thing from you: scare you beyond anything you can ever imagine, and send you home so shaken up sleep is unachievable. People pay to be petrified and scared to death. Some don't even make it through the haunted houses; the terror seems too real to them.

What if instead of waiting until October's newest scary haunted house to walk through, your own home was that living nightmare? No actors, no props; just a safe place you once called home, the safe place that's no longer your safe haven. Every single night, you would pray for daylight to come faster, terrified to open your eyes at night and witness something so unimaginable it would send a scream ripping out of your throat.

I used to search for that haunted house every October until that haunted house became my own.

"Becca? Becca? Earth to Becca," I hear my name and realize that I'm in our car looking out the passenger window in a complete daze.

"What are you thinking about?" Mitch asks.

"Nothing, just some random thought!" An uncomfortable sigh comes out.

"Well, what you should be thinking about are these houses we've seen, we have just one left and one of them has to be our next home."

Mitch and I met 21 years ago in the one place they say you would never meet the forever one, in a nightclub. Boy, did we show them. A strong marriage and two beautiful sons together; having the love of my life as my best friend made it that much better.

Looking out the car window, I brush my hand through my hair.

"I'm so tired of moving and unpacking and packing again. Promise me this is the last one for a while."

Due to Mitch's job, we have been moving every one to two years for the last ten years. I feel lucky to have such an amazing husband with a great job; it allows us to have the lifestyle we want to live with our boys. The only price we pay is relocating where they need him, whenever they need him. My son Connor is seven, and Logan is almost four and a half. To them, the constant moving around is exciting with new rooms and new bedroom themes. Of course, the pool and hot tub are icing on the chocolate cake — a whole new adventure for small boys with tons of energy.

"Listen, I don't like moving either, but this one should be the last one for a while. All we have to do is find the right one here in Dallas."

We have been all over North Texas, and the heat index is through the roof. At this point, I'm just about done looking. Any house would be good just to end the search. I love Texas: the people and the country lifestyle are my favorite part. Being a country girl at heart brought up on a farm, so Texas feels a little like a home away from home.

"Here it is." Mitch says.

We pull into a golf course community entrance with a very well-manicured property. Then drive past two outdoor community pools and parks. There are kids playing on the streets and families riding golf carts in their neighborhood. It looks nice, but I'm not sold yet. Unfortunately, the time of year to look for a rental with what we need doesn't leave much to desire. It doesn't help that the housing market is at an all-time low with not many choices available. Either a great house with a low-rating school or the other way around. We have no time to wait on what else would come on the market; this is it. We have to move in four weeks, and so far, it looks like nothing is leaning in our favor. I want to buy a home to put our roots down, but something inside me is uncertain about how long we will be here. History has a funny way of not giving me a sense of settling down and growing old in one spot anytime soon.

After driving through the community, we finally pulled into the driveway of 1220 Greenway Close.

"Well, it has a nice curb appeal and a double garage!" I say.

"That's the spirit, Becca. Let's go take a look."

"Wake the boys up, all this driving has them napping which is completely out of the ordinary for them."

Gently, my hands stroke their sweet little faces. "Boys, last house. Let's stretch our legs".

They open their sleepy eyes. "Are we here? Yay! Logan, let's go see!"

The boys are fully charged again as they shoot out from the back at rocket speed. Logan needs a bit of assistance to keep up with his older brother. We step out of the car to see William, our realtor and family relocation specialist, hired by Mitch's company. William has been a realtor for quite some time and is hoping to finally retire next month. Looking tired, William gets out of his car, and he walked up the driveway at a slow pace as if every step was exhausting for him.

"This is the last one today. Master bedroom down, three bedrooms up with kids living area, two and a half bathrooms, fire place, pool and a school down the street with a 9/10 rating."

"Sounds good," Mitch says, "This could be the one." He looks over at me with a wink and smile.

I can't help but smile back. He's so cheesy but always optimistic—a true kid at heart.

William unlocks the front door, and the boys push past him to get in first.

"Unlike the others, this one is vacant and has been for some time."

"Why is that?" I ask. The smell of fresh paint and carpet hit me as if it was just done yesterday, not to mention how hot it is with no air movement for God-knows-how-long.

"Not sure!" William continues. "Could be because a company looks after it for the original owner; it can sometimes be a pain with getting things fixed or looked at. You have a whole process for everything. You have to call in, create a ticket and so on and so forth."

We walk around the first floor and look around while positively commenting on the wide-open concept. The living room has floor-to-ceiling windows with a nice view of the sparkling blue pool in the backyard. We open the back door and step out onto the deck.

"Babe, look at this outdoor kitchen, it wasn't even mentioned!" Mitch fumbles through the papers.

"Yeah I see, crazy." I look around and inspect everything. "So how long has this been vacant?"

Williams is fast to reply, "It says here… just around eight months."

"This price, and it hasn't been rented? Is something wrong with it?" The rental price is $700 lower than the others we looked at today, and they were much older than this one.

"No, I don't think so," replies William. "I think it's just the application process that's usually a pain; a big deterrent!"

Leaving the men to talk, I start heading inside and down the hall. Upstairs to the left side, the boys are already loving the open empty space playing tag. "Settle down, boys, let's not get carried away."

The banister looks over the front door entrance and not far from the first bedroom. I step into the rather small room on the right side of the top of the stairs and walk across to the window. The window looks down on the neighbor's side of the house, and it was noticeable how close we are to the next home. A creaking sound is behind me. I turn around and see the bedroom door slowly closing shut.

"Boys?" I frown, not sure why the door closed with no windows open. Even the air conditioner hasn't been on for

6

some time. *Must be the kids,* I think to myself. A crisp cool draft comes from what feels like the floor going up my legs, instantly feeling head-to-toe goosebumps. With the coolness on my face, my whole body shutters. Looking around for the vent, I notice it's on the other side of the room, on the left side of the ceiling. I felt a rather unsettling feeling; my hair gently moves as if a small fan is blowing in the room. I head for the door that has now closed completely shut. The door handle is as cold as ice, almost stinging my hand. The door opens fine, and I'm somewhat relieved as my mind starts racing to the moments in question. "Odd how cold that doorknob was," I say out loud while looking down at my hand.

Everyone downstairs is obviously having fun as they finish exploring the house. Heading to the top of the stairs, I start to make my way down to the first landing. Overtaken by a powerful sensation to look behind me, I try to resist. *Look, look now!* I scare myself and lose my footing; I stumble on the last stair and look back to see nothing was behind me. Leaving me with an uneasy feeling, I continue down the hall with a little speed to my step to reach my family, not wanting to look back again.

Everyone is now making their way out the front door in deep discussion.

"So... what do you think? I love it! It's newly renovated, a great school close by and the golf course is a huge bonus." Mitch motions driving a ball.

"Like I said, it can be rather a pain with another company versus the actual home owner, the last house we viewed was okay too!" says William, steering us away from this house again. "We should go," William motions me to join him outside.

"Has anything happened in this house in the past?"

"Ohh, here we go!" Mitch laughs. "Excuse my wife, William, she asks this every single time we find a house. She's asking you if anyone has died in this house. Any ghosts in the attic?" With a nod and with a little embarrassment, I pipe up, "Yes, I find it odd this house hasn't sold and is now being rented well below cost, yet still has no movement." *Not to mention what I felt upstairs, but I'll keep that to myself.*

William looks rather uncomfortable and maybe a little shocked at the straightforward question. "No, absolutely not! No one has died in this house.

Does he really have to tell us the truth? He didn't even look into the question, and I doubt it says no one has died in this house on his paper in front of him. We are just renters, not homeowners.

William locks the door behind me as I step outside. Standing there, I pay a quick stare at the front of the house. "Well, I'm sold!" Mitch says. "We lucked out with this house and I say we jump on it now."

"I don't know, Mitch, there's something about it, and we don't need to jump on it, it's been listed forever."

"Well, should we sign some papers for the last house?" William suggests.

"Nope, this is the one, let's do this… right honey?" Mitch continues.

I say nothing while we buckle the kids in the back seat of the rental car.

"I love this house, Mom," says Connor. "It's beautiful, can we live here, please?"

We get in the car and back out of the driveway. I look up at the dark windows on the second floor, contemplating what I felt upstairs. *Am I just being silly? It was a little creepy.*

Then, for a split second, it seems as if a dark figure from the corner of the window was looking right down at me. He was standing in the bedroom I was just in. I don't think I was alone in that room.

CHAPTER 2

The moving truck rolls up to 1220 Greenway Close, brakes screeching to a halt. If there's anything to announce to this street, it's that this house has finally been rented, and our moving truck is almost blocking the entire road as we start unloading. Thank goodness there's another exit for people to drive out of. We open the front door to let the movers start bringing in our belongings. The children are over the moon with excitement, but not me. After what I experienced and thought I saw while we pulled away a month ago, uneasiness was still a constant feeling for me. That haunting image of a figure at the window is burned in my memory.

The kids are running straight for the back to hit the pool, so I follow, carrying Mats, my two-pound Chihuahua. I don't want to be in the way of the chaos of boxes or think about anything supernatural when I have to sleep here starting tonight.

"Boys are excited, huh?" says Mitch. "We should just get the beds ready and have some easy dinner tonight." Mitch says while bending over, petting Mats.

"Yep, sounds good," I reply.

A couple of hours later, our new house starts to calm down when the movers finally wrap things up, and the boys wind down on the couch, coloring. I head over to the open front door

11

to wave thanks to the movers for all their help. Getting ready to close the door, a group of women is standing in front of our house on the sidewalk, talking amongst themselves and looking right at me. Not sure what's going on or what to think as I stand there. As I waved, the only thing my voice can get out with a slightly confused look was a "Hi!" The lady leading the group steps forward, and the others straggle behind. "Hi, my name is Carol, and I live next door." She points to the house I had previously admired from the bedroom upstairs. "We just wanted to see for ourselves that someone has moved into this house".

Is this a welcoming committee?

"Yes, my family and I are excited to move into this house and community."

"You have two boys? In this house? Oh, sorry… What I mean is… I have two children as well who would love to meet your little ones."

In this house? What is this lady talking about? She sounded almost appalled.

"Well, anyways… We will let you get settled. We all live in this neighborhood and are very happy to see this house finally rented after so long. We also brought you dinner assuming you would need a break after such a long day. Welcome to the neighborhood," Carol says, handing over a bag with a rotisserie chicken and salads.

"Oh my, you didn't have to do this," I say, shocked and grateful. "I thought this only happened in movies, Texas hospitality at its best." I smile.

"You're very welcome, we will see you around." Just like that, the group of ladies dispersed and walked away. I was left standing at the door thinking to myself, *what just happened?*

Closing the door behind me, Mitch grabs the paper plates from the bag.

"Wow, they thought of everything, even cutlery! What a great neighborhood!"

"Yeah," I reply. "That was so nice of them."

After a very long day, we are all exhausted. The beds in each room are already made. Moving the family so much in the past few years is enough to know the first day is exhausting, and the top priority is rest. The boys' rooms are side by side, one of them being the small room looking over Carol's backyard. I first tuck Logan in. "Goodnight, my love, sleep tight."

As I'm sitting beside him, tucking the blankets in, uneasiness about the new room is clearly what he is feeling. New sounds and boxes can definitely make it less cozy, so I make sure to illuminate his room with the nightlight that gives the underwater projection on the walls and ceiling. Logan loves it and always has since he was a baby. He watches the ceiling projection for a second and then closes his eyes. I get up quietly and glance at my precious baby one more time. Closing the door halfway, then I head to Connor's room; no chance to say goodnight as he's in a deep slumber already. I turn off the light, close the door halfway as well, and start heading for the stairs. The stairs bring a flashback of the feeling of someone behind me when I first viewed this house. Walking down, I'm quite relieved I feel nothing. With a deep sigh of relief, I head to our master room on the first floor.

I get changed and crawl into bed with my entire body exhausted and sore. "This is going to be a great move, I can feel it," Mitch says while crawling into bed and wrapping his arms around me. A new chapter.

At 3:39 am, I'm sitting up, listening, and looking around, remembering where I am. In the new house. What is that sound? *Maybe it's nothing; maybe it's just me.* Not long after the pause, movement above me agitates me. What the heck is that? It sounds like it's coming from upstairs. Is it the boys? The movement has now moved in the living room not far from our bedroom door. Now I hear the shuffling right outside our door in the hallway. Then silence. Complete silence. All I can hear is my breathing and Mitch's slight snoring. I sit frozen, straining to listen, realizing I'm struggling to exhale. *Is it my boys?* Thoughts pass through my mind again. A creaking sound of our doorknob turning makes me gasp, as the sudden full force of our door props open and bounces off the wall, and to almost slam shut again. My heart jumps out of my chest. Mitch shoots right up from deep sleep to the upright position. "What's that? What's going on?" We both look at the door to see a small little human holding his teddy. It's sweet, Logan.

"Mommm… I can't sleep, there's someone in my room, a zombie!" I get up and scoop him in our bed right between us.

"Son, I can guarantee you there's no zombie in your room; it's just a new house, new sounds… you can sleep here tonight," assures Mitch.

Logan closes his eyes, and Mitch wraps his arms around our son. It almost seems like they are already drifting off to sleep. The conversation has stopped. With my heart still racing, I try to calm down, thinking if there was something in his room. *Could it have something to do with the thing I thought I saw? No, what am I thinking? This is just a new house, and it's going to take some getting used to for sure.* My head is now on the soft pillow, and I look over to see Logan already in a deep sleep. Closing my own eyes, the silence of the house drifts me off to sleep not far behind them.

The sun starts to come up and shine, with the first bit of orange and pink showing in our room. It's a beautiful thing to wake up to. The reflection of the sun hitting the water projects dancing lights on our bedroom ceiling. It's so peaceful. My body is sore, and a good stretch is always enjoyable. I grab my housecoat to head down the hall and leave the boys to continue the well-deserved little sleep. Heading into the kitchen, I'm extremely grateful I unpacked the coffee maker yesterday. Today would be a coffee day, all day long. Plus, nothing starts my morning like fresh coffee beans brewing and filling the house with the aroma of pure heaven. I pour myself a coffee in my oversized mug and head outside to the backyard to enjoy peace and quiet before the craziness of children and unpacking begins. This moment is the perfect Mommy time.

"Good morning, beautiful." I look over to see Mitch stepping outside with a coffee in his hand.

"Good morning. Did you sleep okay?"

"You mean after Logan gave me complete heart failure with the door launching open in the middle of the night? I was in a deep sleep when that happened, but fell back asleep right away once our little buddy snuggled in."

"Yeah, he gave me a heart attack too, those zombies!" A little chuckle exists in my mouth. "Logan clearly hears stories from his older brother."

Mitch bends over to kiss me. "Well, we have a busy day. TV, Internet and alarms are all being done today with the first person arriving in ten minutes, so let's get cracking."

He is right; it's time to get started. I head in, get changed, and ready to tackle the big mess of boxes. The doorbell rings, and we are off to the races with Grand Central Station of activity. Mitch gets the door and lets a man into the house, clearly looking like the TV and internet installer with his company logo on his shirt. "Morning, ma'am," he says with a nod of the head. Mitch shows him around to the hookup locations. I turn around to see my little Logan rubbing his eyes and walking towards me.

"Mom?" he says.

"Let's get your brother up and get you both dressed!"

"Can we go in the pool first?" My boys were born with gills pure-water babies.

"How about right before lunch?"

"Okay," he replies.

Easy morning negotiations at its finest, I giggle. Both boys are up and eating cereal, with Connor bragging at how well he slept, "Like a baby, Mom."

Logan pipes up and says, "Not me, I had a zombie standing in the middle of my room and he was just staring at me."

"What?!" Connor seems concerned and instantly stops shoveling cereal in his mouth.

"No one had anything in their room!" I interrupt. "It's just a new house and will take some getting used to. You will see, it's perfectly fine."

Right? I think to myself. *Positive.* Last move and this house is perfect. Completely perfect.

The doorbell goes again. Heading to the front door, I open it to see Carol standing there with two boys who look to be the same age as mine. "Good morning, Becca. I don't mean to bother you when I'm sure you're in the middle of unpacking, but I thought I could have the boys over to play with mine. This is Jacob and Michael." She taps them on the shoulders. "This way it can give you a bit of time to get settled and get some unpacking done with no interruptions. Mine are just itching to play with yours."

"Oh… Umm, yeah sure… Yeah, that's totally fine."

"Yay! Mom, can we show them our rooms?!" Connor asks while tugging at my shirt with excitement. Connor has always been a social boy ever since he was born. He has always been making friends and having endless playdates. Something I always enjoyed doing too.

"Oh, no! My boys don't need to go in there. Oh, I mean while it's all crazy with boxes. Let's have you over to my house, we have a trampoline and a new puppy in the backyard!"

Once again, the weird vibe that she doesn't like my house is back. "Yes, no problem. Let me know if you need anything, or I can come over while they play," I suggest.

"I got this. Happy unpacking." Carol winks, then off she goes next door with all the kids full of excitement. I close the door and look at the house from the doorway.

Yeah, maybe it is a maze of boxes. I tie my hair back, and I open the first box of many. *Let's do this.*

"I don't understand. How is that possible? This makes no sense!" I hear Mitch in the other room rather angry an hour later. I walk in to see Mitch rubbing his head in confusion.

"What's going on?" I ask.

"They say there is no copper in the walls of this house, and this has to be done to get everything running."

"What? That makes no sense!"

"I know! He's calling someone else that can help get things done, but we are looking at a good delay in everything now!"

"Great!" I said sarcastically in complete disbelief and relieved the kids are at the neighbor's and not here upset they can't play their games or watch Netflix on their iPads. I head outside in our backyard to hear the boys all playing together in Carol's backyard. The squealing of pure laughter and new friends makes me feel so happy amongst all this mess. It is promising to have a nice neighbor who especially wants to lend a hand.

"Becca, that's not just it either!" Mitch storms outside with a phone to his ear. "I'm on hold with the rental company for this house. We have no pool heater on the side of the house, just an empty space."

"What?" I say in complete confusion. The heater for the pool and hot tub were completely removed. "It was here four weeks ago, wasn't it?" I ask.

"I have no idea, this is a complete mess and now I've been on the phone with this stupid rental company for this house explaining the problem, and they have the nerve to say it's not mandatory!" Mitch is getting more and more upset by the minute.

"Not mandatory?" I whisper to myself. "That's ridiculous!"

"Listen, this backyard has a pool and hot tub, it's not a bloody pond. This is false advertising, and these items were here before, so they need to come back now!" Mitch screams into the phone. Good grief, here we go; let's just add to the craziness. Thank God I'm a professional unpacker and have managed to bang out almost all the first-floor boxes. Then, the doorbell rings again.

CHAPTER 3

A rather short older lady in an oversized sundress is at my door.

"Hi!" I say while watching the lady staring at me.

"Oh, sorry. I was shocked the door opened. There hasn't been anyone in the house here for a very long time. I heard backyard noises from my house. We share a back fence."

"We moved in yesterday."

"We?" The lady questions.

"Yes, my husband and two kids."

"Oh… I see!" She says with a concerned tone.

What is with every one and this house? Yes, we have moved here. We know it's been empty, and I'm right in the middle of dealing with a complete nightmare of things that have all gone wrong in just a couple of hours, so what do you need?

"Since there's someone in this house now, I should tell you about the rats."

"Rats?" I say with a shocked tone of voice.

"This house has been empty, and it pours out such a negative energy that rats have been attracted to it. It is infesting our neighborhood."

"I can assure you… I'm sorry your name was?"

"It doesn't matter what my name is, I didn't give it to you. I'm just telling you your rats are running along the fence line and I've called this company." She points to the lease rental sign leaning up against the house. "They need to do something about it, and they won't".

"I will look into this and thanks so much for coming over and checking on the house," I say.

She lets out a snort in the air from her nose and turns her back to me as she starts to walk away. "Bye now," I say while closing the door.

"Who was that?" Mitch asks.

"Some crazy lady said we have rats; she was so rude."

"I was going to call an exterminator anyway just to look and spray for the fire ants too." Living in Texas has shined some light on exterminators; they are our best friends.

"We have someone here now doing the wiring and the hot tub heater should be going in within a couple of days," Mitch continues.

"What a draining first day! I'm going to run next door and get the boys." I head out our front door, leaving Mitch to start breaking down the unpacked boxes. I walk up Carol's driveway, and I ring the doorbell.

"Becca, come on in. The kids are having so much fun they can stay longer, and I can make hot dogs for dinner."

"Awe, thanks Carol, you are kind, but we are going to get cleaned up and explore some restaurants in the area for dinner. You have helped so much with the kids today."

The boys run to the door, begging to stay longer.

"Nope, not today, we are going to go out for dinner." I help them put on their shoes.

"You know, Becca, I didn't want to come off strange with the group introduction yesterday. The whole street was buzzing. The house was rented, and we were so happy it was going to be filled with a happy family. I look at your house next door everyday being vacant and almost sad. I'm so glad you and your family are here." She touches my arm.

"Thanks Carol, we are happy to be here. Thanks again." I usher the boys out. Carol stood at the door with an almost sad smile on her face. *Thank goodness this long day is coming to an end.*

We head out for dinner and enjoy a rather delicious Mexican restaurant not far from us. The boys love fajitas; they would eat them every day if they could. Pulling back into our driveway, I don't even look at the second-floor window, not wanting to feed back into my imagination.

"I'm so glad this day is over," Mitch says. "It was complete hell. How about we take these sleepy heads upstairs to bed and watch the Redbox movie I grabbed?"

The boys must have played hard at Carol's. They were fast asleep in their seats. The ten-minute drive from the restaurant knocked them out.

"Sounds good," I reply.

Mitch unlocks the front door, and the lights from inside the house illuminate our entry.

"I thought we turned the lights off," I said.

"I guess you didn't." He shrugs as he carries Logan upstairs, with sleepy Connor walking not far behind. *I swear I turned them all off, didn't I?* I head up the stairs to kiss both boys goodnight starting with Logan's room.

Logan wakes up from his sleep and completely freaks out, kicking his hands and feet. "Nooooo! I'm not sleeping in here; he's going to come back! I want to sleep with Connor."

"Yeah, Mom, can we have a sleepover tonight? I want him to sleep in my bed," Connor yells from his room. Connor had taken our old queen bed, so he was excited to have his brother sleeping in his big boy bed with him.

"Okay, then! Tonight only." I'm the worst negotiator. We tuck them both in and turn the lights off. Mitch heads downstairs to put on the movie, and as I start to descend the stairs, I stop and look towards Logan's bedroom as the door slowly creaks closed on its own. Choosing to ignore it completely, I walk straight downstairs, not looking back. We have the air conditioner on, or maybe there's just something wrong with that door.

Mitch and I snuggle up to watch the Redbox movie, and I fall asleep 30 minutes into it. Mitch nudges me awake not long after I doze off, smiling, knowing he busted me not making it through a movie, yet again. Admitting defeat to falling asleep on the couch, I head to our bedroom, crawling into bed rather fast, wanting to chase my deep sleep I just minutes ago achieved. Mitch crawls in not long after me, and I have a feeling he feels the same after such an exhausting day.

Many hours later, the sound of "Mom... Dad..." whispered in our room again, and it woke me up. Sitting up, I adjust my eyes to the darkness of the room and glance at the alarm clock. It reads 3:39 am. "Logan?" I look around. The fan blowing on high is moving my hair slightly. Our bedroom door is wide open. Since we sleep with our door closed, I know Logan is in here somewhere. Once again, I call out "Logan?"

My eyes start to adjust to the darkness a bit more, and I notice Logan is standing behind the open door, almost tucked in between the wall and the door. "Logan? What's wrong, baby?" He is whimpering and playing with the door handle turning it open and close, making a clicking sound with each twist over and over. He's not responding to me; he is just playing with the door handle. I shake Mitch.

"Mitch, turn on your lamp. Logan is here upset." Mitch stirs out of sleep and fumbles for the lamp, knocking other items off the nightstand in the process. A burst of light illuminates the entire room, not leaving a single shadow.

"Where?" asks Mitch. Looking towards the door and there's no one there.

Is Logan gone? "What? He was just there, I saw him."

Mitch gets up to use the washroom and says, "I think you were dreaming."

My heart starts racing, but I heard him whispering our names. I grab my housecoat and walk through the open bedroom door and past the living room. *Maybe he ran back upstairs?* I'm nervous and can feel my palms start to sweat with anxiety. I turn on the living room lights, and I call out, "Logan?" Nothing. Checking to the front door where the stairs to the second-floor start, the lights are all off; Logan would have turned them all on to see. I turn on the hall lights and walk up towards Connor's room. Their bedroom door is closed, just how I left it. With my hand on the doorknob, I slowly turn it to the right, and gently pushing the door open.

My heart is now beating out of my chest. The door is open enough to place my head in and peak. Connor and Logan are fast asleep. A gasp gets out, and I take a step back, feeling the hair on the back of my neck stand up. The hall starts to spin, and my hand is on the wall to stabilize myself. *I know what I saw and what I heard.* I pull myself together, take a deep breath, and close the door quietly. As I was walking away from Connor's room towards the landing, I noticed Logan's bedroom door closed. A blue light was shining from underneath his door, recognizing the colors right away. It's from his night light projection lamp. I only turn on when I tuck him in. My hands reach the railings to the first stair.

Suddenly, feeling light-headed again, the room starts to spin, and my body heats up with nausea. Then, a child's giggle erupts from Logan's room and I know that's not my son.

"Logan must have left this on," Mitch says, and he passes me coming up the stairs and heading to Logan's room. His voice breaks me out of the shock I was feeling, and the room suddenly stops abruptly spinning around me. Mitch turns the doorknob, opens Logan's door, walks right in, and turns off the night light. Following behind him slowly, I approached the room to see no one; nothing to explain the child's giggling coming from the room moments ago. Speechless, I stand in the center of the room with a blank look on my face.

"Kids asleep?" Mitch asks. "Hello? Kids asleep?"

"Umm, yes," I respond, snapping out of this uncertain moment. Then, heading downstairs in disbelief, I leave Mitch following behind.

27

"Looks like you were the one dreaming tonight," he laughs as he wraps his arm around my shoulders. "Come on, let's get some sleep."

Letting out a fake smile in agreement, however, I know sleep is out of the question tonight after this.

CHAPTER 4

Exhausted is not a strong enough word for how I feel this morning. There isn't enough coffee I can ingest that can possibly give me the extra kick needed. This is my third cup, and absolutely nothing is giving me the energy needed. Today we must head over to the new school with our proof of registration and take a private tour with the kids. Connor is excited for his first day at school, and the boys are playing nicely this morning. I dread breaking it up. This uninterrupted time is much needed, a moment to replay last night. Putting my coffee cup down, I start to head up to Logan's room. The door is open from the boys running in and out of it, with the light shining brightly from the window giving it an inviting and pleasant feeling during the day. It's hard to imagine the fear in this room hours ago. As I am glancing at my watch, I realize that it's time to get the boys to put on their shoes and head out the door.

We take the kids to the elementary school and are very pleased with the staff and teachers. The school was built just a few years ago and still has the new-school smell. Logan will be going to a preschool two days a week to make some new friends; he's not at the age to join his brother in elementary school yet, but it's a great time to take baby steps towards socializing and being away from mom. It works well because it gives me the time to run errands and get some uninterrupted cleaning time done. After signing the kids up for their new schools, we head back home with the plan of hitting the pool. One great thing about Texas is that the sun is always shining, making everything that much better. It was always overcast and dreary at our last home in Canada, and let's face it, everyone needs some sunshine. It is the kind of change we can all take advantage of with a cool dip in the pool and the sun on our back.

As I was opening the front door, kids blast past me heading straight upstairs to get changed for the pool. In the meantime, I grab the towels and some juice boxes for extra hydration. I open the back door, and as I'm standing in front of the pool, I yell, "What on earth is that? Mitch?" pointing into the pool.

Floating at the surface of the entire pool are what look like strings of balls.

"Is it a plant of some sort?" Mitch steps out towards the pool. "What the heck is that?". He grabs the pool net and gets underneath the strand; the black balls float in every direction. "They are eggs of some sort, the whole pool is full of them."

"This is gross, I'm calling the exterminator right now. I want to know what the heck this is." I grab my phone.

30

"Let's get a pool company here too to clean this all up, I've never seen anything like this, there must be millions."

The kids come running out, ready to dive into the pool. Mitch stops them right before Connor's leap.

"Nope, boys, not today. The pool has something yucky in it. Let's head over to the neighborhood pool. We can go for a walk."

"Can we play on the playground too?" begs Logan.

"We sure can," I say. Relieved, we have a good and close backup plan until we get this looked at. Disgusting.

After playing in the sun for a couple of hours, the boys are now down for an afternoon nap. The exterminator we called has pulled up in front of our house in his work truck. I get to the door before he rings the bell to avoid waking the boys from a much-needed slumber.

"Ma'am," he says, "I'm going to get started outside and then take a peek inside for you, I'll let you know what I find."

"Thanks so much," I say, happy he's here to take a deep dive in and around our house.

I start doing the last of moving around the furniture in the living room and move some lamps over to their closet outlet, placing them on the end tables. As I was reaching up to turn on the lamp, I realize there's no knob, just the screw to where the knob once was. Frowning, I start looking around the table and on the floors, to find nothing. I also reached for the other lamp and noticed the knob is missing on this one too. "What the?"

I walk over to the hall lamp to peek under to see if the knob is missing too. Every single lamp in our house has no knobs to turn on anymore. "This is weird!" I mumble to myself. "If it was pitch black and we needed immediate light, it could be a dangerous situation." "Who would do this?" I say out loud.

Mitch has a home office located by the front door; he strolls out of his office,

"I'm so busy today, what's going on with all these lamps in the hallways?"

"Honestly, I don't know, every single one of them is missing the knob to turn it on."

"That is weird. No big deal, I have to run to Home Depot later, I can see if they have some knobs that would work. Maybe they fell off during the move."

"Yeah, maybe," I said. *But not likely, they have to be screwed off,* I thought.

A knock at the front door catches my attention. When I open it, our exterminator is there. "I'm all done outside, and it looks like we have some problems. The pool is full of toad eggs; I located a couple on the side of the house. What's crazy is the amount in your pool; you would think you had hundreds of toads on your property. You also have a couple fire ant mounds which I took care of and you do have evidence of rats."

"Are you serious? Can we take care of all of this today?"

"Yes, no problem. We will also make sure to put some bate boxes out and check on it every visit; it's all echo friendly."

"Alright, let's do it."

He slips on his shoe covers. "I'm just going to take a look around the inside and then I'm all done."

"Sounds good! The boys are sleeping in the far left room upstairs, so if you don't mind not waking them."

"I have kids of my own and don't worry, I won't. Mine are grumpy when woken up." He chuckles.

"Thanks!" I respond.

The exterminator leaves the driveway while the pool guys have now come and gone. He gave the pool a good clean, removing the toad eggs, and shocked the pool. He let us know swimming was not an option anytime soon. The pool heater was also installed on the side of the house and made it that much more disappointing not being able to give it a try right away. It seems so much is going on with our house in the last couple of days. All I want is a good hot soak in the hot tub, hoping all this craziness is coming to an end soon.

The boys ate dinner fast as it was their favorite, spaghetti. Quiet time was fast approaching. I loved what we called quiet time growing up. It usually started around 8-8:30 pm and always meant a soft light snuggled in with a good book. I crawl into the bed with the boys and read them their favorite book, the pout-pout fish. I can read this book over and over, and they would never get tired of it. Logan is sleeping in Connor's room again, and I'm okay with it. School doesn't start for a couple more days, and I love how close the boys are. After finishing the book, they are both sound asleep, and I quietly sneak out of the room. Heading down the hallway, walking past Logan's door, I notice it is wide open and is as dark as spades. Everything seems quiet, almost normal. Making my way down the stairs and into our master bedroom, I get ready for bed, slipping into some very comfy pajamas.

"I can't get over all the things going on with this house, it's never ending."

"Well, there's more!" Mitch says. "I had the electrician take a look around and he found a couple dead outlets and some pool lights that aren't working."

"What?" I say in frustration. "Mitch, this is ridiculous. How safe is this house? Is everything even up to code? I just read an article yesterday about a poor child being electrocuted by a bad pool light in their own pool."

"I know," Mitch responds. "I've already called the rental company and created another ticket to get this home inspected from top to bottom. Someone should be out here next week."

"Next week?!"

"Yes, it's the process with this company. They find another contractor and that person calls us to schedule and then they come out."

I'm so annoyed; words struggle to get out.

"This house is safe, they wouldn't have rented it out of it wasn't," Mitch continues.

"Seems like a lot of crap for our first couple weeks, Mitch!"

"What do you want me to do? Should we move again?" He snaps back.

If only it were that simple. I crawl into bed and close my eyes. This is starting to turn into a little much.

***

Hours later, I woke up. It's dark, and something must've woken me. Waiting for my eyes to adjust, the moonlight from my window is in the room, and I listen closely. Mitch is heavily breathing. He usually snores; with his asthma, he tends to make a lot of noises while sleeping, especially if his allergies flare up. With my back to him, I listen to his breathing and almost gurgling. *At least he's getting some sleep*, I think to myself. Sounds of toads talk back and forth. So much for the exterminator relocating all of them, it sounds like a colony is outside. I continue to listen to Mitch breathing so heavy, and I'm desperate for sleep. *Maybe I should make him roll over.*

I turn over to wake him, and I freeze. The little light in the room is bending around a small dark figure on Mitch's side of the bed, just inches from his sleeping body. While my eyes continue to adjust, more characteristics come to light. It's not my child. This child has short blonde hair and very pale skin with dark circles under those sunken jet black eyes that are as cold as death. The child's gaze is locked straight on Mitch. He is just staring and not blinking. His light-colored T-shirt is filthy and far too big because he's so thin and frail, with almost grey-tinted skin on his tiny skeletal frame. He tilts his head slightly like he's studying Mitch, and the slow gurgling breathing I thought was Mitch was not. It was coming from this boy by our bed.

The child slowly lifts his left hand and reaches towards Mitch's face. Not realizing I'm completely holding my breath frozen in fear, a scream violently erupts from my lungs. Reaching for Mitch, I frantically grab at him, trying to pull him towards me, away from the cold, pale hand of this boy. The scream breaks the child's gaze, and he starts to look right at me, making complete eye contact. Mitch awakens, screaming in agonizing pain. "What the hell! My back!" The boy disappears with his last gaze on me.

"Oh my God, Mitch, there was someone…"

"My back!" Mitch screams again in agony. He shoots out of bed, throws the blankets off of him, and turns on the bathroom light. My body jumps out of bed after him and into the bathroom; my eyes grow big. I look at Mitch's back, and there is blood, a lot of blood.

"What the hell did you do to my back?"

"I had a dream you were falling, babe, I was reaching for you pulling you towards me away from the…" *I'm not about to tell him an unknown boy was about to touch his face. What if I was really dreaming this?* I scramble to help him and grab a towel.

"Look at my back! This hurts!" It looks like a wolverine shredded his back. The marks are deep enough to bleed constantly, and now blood is slowly dripping down his back and onto the floor.

"I'm so sorry, I feel horrible. Here, let me help you." I grab another damp cloth and help clean up the open wounds on his back. The first aid kit from the closet is now in my hands. Frantically, I open it and grab some gauze and bandages. Hot tears burn in my eyes, and my throat feels like it is closing, holding back everything to prevent from sobbing

37

uncontrollably. *What have I done?* I was trying to save my husband. Instead, I caused him pain and feel sick to my stomach. Mitch can see the heartache and worry in my eyes. He winces in pain as he crawls into bed after his back is bandaged up.

"Damn, babe, your dreams are crazy."

"I know, I'm so sorry." I can't even cuddle up to him because his raw bandaged back is facing me, unable to touch the sheets. I close my eyes as questions run through my head. *What have I done? What did I see? What is going on?*

***

The morning light shines into our room, and I haven't slept a wink. The last image burning into my memory is of those empty black eyes of the child. He was a young boy around the age of seven or eight, and when he looked up at me, it was almost as if he was startled by my scream, shocked that I could see him.

Mitch steps out of the room, "I can't even have a shower. When water hits my back, it kills me!"

"Mitch, I feel terrible! I'm so sorry."

The kids come running down the stairs seconds after bursting into our room. "Daddy, look at your back! Did a tiger attack you?"

"Yes!" Mitch says with a wink looking at me. I let out a half-smile but don't feel like this is something to smile about.

"Mommy accidentally scratched Dad in his sleep."

The boys turn their heads toward me with their mouths wide open in shock.

"Mommmy! You're not sleeping with me anymore!"

The boys giggled.

"Oh, stop!" I roll my eyes. "Let's go have some breakfast." I usher them out of the room.

"Good news, boys. The pool is clean and as blue as the sky. I have some water guns that could use some practicing." Mitch hands two water blasters over.

"Yahhhhh!" the kids scream, jumping up and down in excitement.

We spent a good couple of hours in the pool, and later I ran some errands with the boys. I feel very distant today, not myself at all. I left Mitch at home with the remainder of the appointments with technicians. Saying the words to them, "Not up-to-code," pushed us up to the top of the list for our tickets; the next couple of days are full of appointments to get the house to where it should have been in the first place. The kids and I get in from all our running around in the Texas heat. I open the front door and see the fans going everywhere, and it's almost as hot inside as outside.

"What on earth?" I say.

"The air conditioner went! Can you believe this?"

"Are you kidding me?"

"I put another ticket in and someone can come out tomorrow. I had to run out and get some fans in the meantime. If it doesn't cool down soon, let's head to a hotel for the night," suggested Mitch.

"Let's cook on the barbecue to avoid heating this house up more and go for an evening swim, it will cool us down in the meantime." I put some groceries on the counter while looking around at all the fans.

Of course, the kids think it's funny. "Look, Mom, it's like a tornado in the house," Connor yells.

"I see that," I respond. *This is such crap. Can anything just go right for once with this house?"*

Mitch cooked some burgers on the barbecue, and the kids swam until they had cute little raisin fingers. They could have played for longer, but I could tell they were ready for sleep.

"I don't think we need to head to a hotel, the house cooled down enough with the blinds closed and the fans running. We should be okay for the night. I put together the kids' beds on my side of the room with soft foam mattress and quilts your mom made, just because it's cooler down here than upstairs."

"Good idea," Mitch says.

The boys giggle in excitement. "A family sleepover!" I tuck them in bed, and not long after, they are fast asleep.

"Their bed looks more comfy than ours," says Mitch. I watch him sit on the edge of the bed with his back facing me, still bandaged up. I put my head on the pillow having flashbacks from last night. Rolling over and turning my back to him, facing the sleeping boys on my side, I can't even look at Mitch's back. Watching them sleep erases my guilt temporarily and brings me pure joy watching them sleep. They look so innocent with not a worry in the world. My eyelids get heavier and heavier, drifting off to sleep.

I stir in the middle of the night, wake up, and look at my dresser to see the time. It is 3:38 am. Glancing over, I can see the boys fast asleep with the reflection of the moon on the pool acting as a nightlight in my own room. Looking at the alarm clock again and watching it turn to 3:39 am. As I am closing my eyes, the sound of the toads talking back and forth is loud enough for me to hear. I am drifting back to sleep, but I can also hear the breathing again—the gurgling. The slow breathing burned into my head from the night before. My muscles couldn't move. My eyes are wide open, frozen in fear. He is here in my room again; I can feel him, not wanting to move an inch. His slow gurgling leaves me frozen in one spot. His breathing is coming from behind me, on Mitch's side of the bed again, where the boy was standing before. *Do I roll over and look? Or ignore it? Maybe it will go away! Please go away; please go away*, I plead in my head.

Grabbing the blankets as tight as possible, I slowly roll over onto my back, turning my head with the slowest of motion. The boy is standing there again, staring at Mitch in the same spot but inches from his face with the same haunting, wilted look from the night before. His head slightly tilted while watching Mitch and observing his sleep. A whimper of fear comes out, and I watch his head slowly go from watching Mitch to my direction. He is now locked on me with those vacant lifeless dark eyes. His pale skin now shows dark spots, areas of rot, and an earthy rancid smell now fills my room, taking my very breath away. Covering my mouth with my hand, I avoid the hot vomit wanting to come up my throat.

My eyes start to water, not wanting to blink for a second because what's next is a mystery. The little boy slowly moves his lips and grins a mischievous evil smile showing his rotten chipped teeth while not breaking eye contact. I push away from Mitch, throwing off my blankets, ready to dive off the bed close to my sleeping boys. I have to protect them. The boy starts to lean over, placing his arms over my sleeping husband. He lifts his left leg onto the bed; he's now crawling over Mitch while he sleeps and making his way to me. With his wicked smile getting larger ear to ear as he creeps closer, he obviously thinks this is a game. The pungent decaying smell coming off of him as he grew closer confirms this is actually happening. He now has someone else to lock onto and play with. He has a plan, and the plan is me.

"Get the hell away from us," I scream and push further away from him with one leg off my bed, not far from my sleeping boys. He continues to crawl completely over Mitch, not disturbing him at all, and doesn't seem phased with me screaming at him to go away. *Why isn't he disappearing?* He's now inches from me, and the overwhelming smell pierces my nostrils. I push away from him, plummeting out of bed and hitting my head on the nightstand, landing a foot away from my sleeping Logan. Now unable to see the top of the bed where he is.

"Oh God, please, please be gone!" I cry to myself from the floor. Standing up, I see the bed area now looks normal, just Mitch still sleeping with his back to me undisturbed. Looking around the room, I do not see the boy anywhere else, but the smell of death lingers just slightly. A couple of minutes go by with me waiting to make sure he is gone, then quietly walk to the bathroom closing the door and rushing to the toilet, throwing up uncontrollably. Wiping my mouth, I sit on the cold tile floor. My entire body is vibrating uncontrollably in shock. *What is happening? What is going on?* I can't wake Mitch up and tell him what I saw; this is the last thing he needs. Tomorrow I need to make a phone call.

CHAPTER 5

"Grandma! Grandpa!" Logan and Connor run up to them on the front lawn. "Boys!" Grandma says as she gets on her knees for great big bear hugs. They almost toppled her over, giggling with excitement. Nothing makes me feel safer than my own mom. Living a country away from them breaks my heart, but no one understands me like my mother.

"Mom," I said and hugged her. The relief just comes pouring out of me; she always has that way with me.

"Someone packed really light." Mitch laughs, bringing in the tiny luggage.

My dad lets out a laugh. "She's planning on shopping down here and buying some new suitcases." My dad leans over for a hug.

Mitch brings the luggage inside and upstairs, and places it in Connor's room. "Are we all having a slumber party?" asks Connor.

"No," responds Mitch. "Grandma and Grandpa can sleep in your room with the big bed and you boys can sleep in Logan's bedroom."

"No way!" screams Connor. "I'm not sleeping in the Zombie Room! I want a sleepover with Grandma and Grandpa!"

"I wish you would stop calling it a Zombie Room, it's definitely not that. Why don't we have a sleepover in our room again?"

"Yeahh!" the boys scream.

"I would like a sleepover in my room too one night," says Grandma.

The boys are now very excited for the double sleepover, and it sounds like fun for everyone. We show my parents the house, and you can tell they are in heaven as soon as they step outside.

"Pool side will be where I'm at," says Grandma.

Mitch has been smoking brisket all day for my parents, and that's one thing he is proud of. Since moving to Texas, we have been exploring good old barbecues, outdoor living, and smoking all kinds of meat. Mitch makes a mean brisket, and the smell of it lingers in the backyard while we bask in the sun. The boys are eager to show the grandparents their new cannonball jumps in the pool and water toys. Grandpa is soon in the pool after them joining in on the boy fun. Since my mom isn't the best swimmer, she's more into sitting in a chair with her feet in the cool, clear water right next to me. The beach entrance to the pool makes it the perfect spot to put a chair and do just that.

"Thanks, Mom, for coming out. It's been a lot to take in!"

"Becca, that's what a mom does, plus I wanted to see my grand babies." She winks.

"It's insane to think about all the things that have gone wrong in this house," Grandpa says from the deep end of the pool. It didn't take long to get him in the warm water.

"You have no idea," says Mitch as he brings out a couple of cold Bud Lights for my parents. My parents are quite young, so it's like having our friends over for a cold one.

"We just had the pool lights done and some rewiring inside the house a couple days ago. We are lucky we didn't get shocked swimming in the pool with the lights out and faulty wiring. The kids have been using the pool almost every day since we moved in."

"That's just annoying and dangerous," replies my mom. "I'm glad everyone is safe and now hopefully settled."

The boys started school, and everything has been a little quiet with less supernatural activity than normal. I haven't seen or heard the boy since that one bad night. I spent countless nights with complete insomnia, scared to sleep but relieved I didn't see him. Nonetheless, he's still here. Every second night or so, Logan's room had the night light come on or random electronic toys turning on and off. I would hear movement upstairs while everyone is at school, but it has become normal for this house. It buzzes with energy but hasn't taken any

47

interest in anyone hearing or seeing him but me. It was something I was now living with and trying to take no notice of. It was becoming *my* normal.

The boys finished the swim and were now finishing up the brisket and homemade potato salad. The recipe was a family favorite past down from my mom and a staple for a backyard barbecue.

"That hit the spot," says Mitch holding his stomach. "Why don't I take the kids and your dad down to the community center by our house to show him the gym? It's a five minute walk and the kids can burn off some energy on the playground too. Let the ladies catch up and give you some mommy time." Mitch leans over for a kiss.

"Sounds good, thanks babe."

Mom and I clean up after dinner. The front door slams shut with their exit, and I sit back outside by the pool with my mom. "So, let's talk about this, Becca. Has anything else happened here since the little boy crawling on the bed?" my mom asks.

"Just the usual stuff now with doors and lights. Sometimes even that's enough. It just gives me the creeps. I know we're not alone in this house, Mom. There's too much stuff going on all the bloody time."

My mom has always had a sense for this kind of stuff, starting when she was a little girl. She grew up having strange dreams or occurrences of faces she never recognized with messages given to her to give to loved ones left behind. Days later, she would see the faces of those people from her dream from accidents that happened on the local news channel. One day, she had a dream of a fireman asking to give a message to his wife. She never understood it until the firefighter's face was on TV the next day as being remembered from a tragic accident the day before thousands of miles away. She never gave those messages to the loved ones, sometimes I don't even think she believed it, but it happened.

"Mom, I tried to pull some research on this house, and I asked the realtor before we moved in if anything had happened here, and he said no. I honestly can't explain what's going on and I definitely can't explain this little boy. It's not random people in a random dream, it's the same boy with the same face in the same clothes, it's weird."

"I don't know what to tell you, Becca. I guess we'll see. There is an eerie feeling upstairs when I go up to the room, but it's also a new house to me. Let's sit back and enjoy each other's company until we figure this all out."

We let out a soft smile to each other and enjoy the sun setting in front of us. *I'm so grateful my mom is here with me. Everything is going to be okay;* I tell myself. Boy was I wrong; it was just about to get started.

49

***

The next morning, I put the coffee on, and not soon after, my mother came around the corner to the kitchen. "How did you sleep?" she asks.

"I actually slept fine, in fact the best I have yet in this house. Must be because you are here." I smile and pass her a fresh cup of coffee. "How did you sleep?"

"I slept okay," she says, but she's not finishing her sentence.

"Okay?"

"I thought I heard the boys up last night, walking and giggling outside of my bedroom door. I got up to look and it was pitch black and silent, they weren't there. I thought maybe they were playing a joke on me." She shrugs.

I say nothing and just maintain eye contact and silence. The best thing about being so close to my mom is sometimes we don't even need to say anything; she just knows what I'm thinking or, in this case, what I'm fearing. When the boys are ready to sleep, they are always down for the count unless they have an accident or a nightmare. I have always been blessed with great sleepers starting at three months old. Down comes my dad breaking the look of concern we are giving each other and letting out a good morning smile. "I slept great. The kids have a very comfortable bed," he says and stretches his arms out.

"That's great, Dad. Hey, today they are having the fall festival in our community with some vendors and some entertainment for the kids like bouncy castles and face painting. I thought we could walk over there this morning before it gets too hot, then spend the afternoon by the pool?"

"That sounds great!" he says.

The kids come running down the stairs straight for the grandparents. "Let's have some fun," Grandma says to the boys.

We arrive back home from the fall festival a couple of hours later, hot and sweaty from spending the entire morning outside in the sun. The boys come tearing into the house with large round red foil balloons. "I'm going to tie my balloon to the chair, Mom, so it doesn't fly away." "That's a great idea, Connor, make sure to do that to your brother's balloon too."

We cool down in the pool, and as the temperature starts to drop down, we fire up the grill. "I'm going to head upstairs and change, Becca. Then help you with dinner." My mother managed to get herself a very good start tan, maybe borderline burn by the pool all afternoon.

"Sure, sounds good," I respond. I start in the kitchen by grabbing the chicken that's been marinating all day to look up and see my mom's panicked face. Her tan is now gone, and she has turned a few shades lighter with a face that says something is terribly wrong.

"Mom?" I ask while putting down the kitchen knife.

"Becca… something is wrong here. I mean, really really wrong."

"Mom, you're scaring me, what do you mean?" I walk over to her, not sure what to expect.

"I got changed in the room and had this horrible feeling. I could feel eyes on my back. It was so bad I looked in the closet to see if the kids were hiding or if dad came upstairs. The feeling was so strong I got changed as fast as I could and went to the landing on top of the stairs. Becca… someone pushed me. I'm not kidding. I felt my back get pushed forward why the rest of my body snapped after. I grabbed the railing and saved myself from flying forward, but I almost flew down the stairs."

"What? Really? Did you slip?" I don't know why I even asked that because I knew my mom didn't slip. This was it; the boy was showing his face again.

"No, I didn't slip, Becca! I was pushed with such force my neck hurts from my head snapping back!"

The guys come in to grab the food for the barbecue. "Mom, don't say anything to anyone, not yet anyways, and I don't want the kids to pick up on this."

Dad came in and grabbed the plate. "What's going on in here, so darn serious?"

"Oh, nothing," my mom says as she puts on a forced smile. Her demeanor has changed now. She understands my dilemma, and it's not just me. She can feel it too, and it's only her second day here.

CHAPTER 6

We eat dinner on the patio and bring everything inside. My mom has not said much since before dinner, and I know she wants to discuss it further. Mitch comes down the stairs into the living room, where we have all just sat down to relax. "Boys are down for the count already. The sun just tires them out."

"That's good," I say. "Let's put on a movie."

"Sure!" Mitch says. I watch him search for a movie on Netflix and happen to look over at my mother. She's just itching to talk to me, but I just can't do it. Now is not the time. The skies are turning pink, and darkness is approaching. Tonight is going to be one of those nights; I can feel it.

The movie starts, and Mitch picks an action-packed show. I'm watching, but nothing's registering. What's noticeable, though, is the rather drastic temperature change in the living room; it's so cold I grab a blanket from the couch and toss another one to my mom. *The air conditioner must be on high, but this is ridiculous.* My mom is looking behind me with a rather strange face. When I turn my head expecting to see one of the boys, I don't. Instead, I see the large ruby red foil balloon floating 4 feet from the floor gliding down the stairs. I look over at my parents, who have both now noticed it.

"The boys' balloon. I thought they tied it up. It will float somewhere and eventually stop, don't worry about it," Mitch says, taking no interest in it.

"I thought it was tied up like the other one," my mom asked.

"Probably just came undone," said my dad, now watching the movie again. My mom, however, is not; she is watching it behind me. I turn to look at it again and notice it's turning a sharp corner from the stairs and now coming straight for us in the living room. It's moving inch by inch slowly as if someone was walking the balloon right to us. It's hard to ignore as it approaches, and I can't help but think this is the perfect height for a child as if they were holding the string. It's not gliding up or down or left or right; it looks like it's being led right toward us.

"What's up with this balloon?" says Mitch with a confused look on his face breaking away again from the movie.

"It's probably following some air current in the house," my dad says, who always has science in his back pocket. He can explain anything rationally.

Aside from vents, there isn't anything that would explain this balloon. I glance over at my mom, and her eyes are getting big with worry. We watch the balloon float perfectly around the coffee table in front of us and stop mid-air in front of the TV, blocking it completely.

"What the?" Mitch gets up to try to swat at the balloon.

My mom pipes up, "No, Mitch, leave it for a second!" she must be curious about what would happen next. The balloon stays in that one spot motionless, frozen, and not budging an inch. We sit awkwardly, just watching it and looking at each other. Mitch sits back down, and we continue to watch the balloon now start moving again back around our table as if someone was now walking away from the living room, and the balloon heads back down the hall.

"I'm sorry everyone, but that's creepy. It literally looks like someone is guiding that balloon with the string walking around the living room table. It's an unnatural movement, balloons just don't do that!"

Mitch lets out a laugh. "That's why I don't watch horror movies, no one is guiding the balloon, it's just a defect, wind current or something else."

I get the same eerie feeling as my mom. My palms are sweating, and my nerves are frazzled; I know what's going on. It's him. My hair is standing up on my arms, and a cool shiver runs down the back of my neck. I turn to look down the hall, and the balloon starts moving again, turning the sharp corner and going back up the stairs. The guys are fully into their movie and not even taking notice of anything else.

My mom whispers to me, "Becca... it went back up the stairs, go see."

I honestly don't want to, but I need to look. Getting up, I walk to the bottom of the stairs and look up. It's not here; it has already turned the corner of the landing, and it's going all the way up to the top of the stairs. I take a couple of more steps, just enough to peek around the corner and see just enough to the top of the staircase. There is the balloon at the very top of the banister not moving, just hovering. That's when the shadow of something standing right next to it is noticeable. Squinting my eyes, I see the pale blonde boy with his veiny white arm holding onto the string of the balloon. Just like we thought, it was being led the whole time; that's why it never fluctuated in height. The boy does a malicious smirk, snaps his head left towards Logan's room, and runs right into it with the foil balloon following behind. I gasp, lose my footing in fright, and stumble down the three stairs I went up. My mom is now on the edge of her seat like she's ready to shoot up as she sees me fall into the hall.

"What on earth did you do?" says Mitch.

I stand up and fix my disheveled self, trying not to look completely crazy. "I...I... just lost my footing, no big deal. It's this maxi dress." I tug at my black dress, acting all frustrated. "It's too damn long." I look back at the stairs and shoot back up them as fast as possible. I make it to the top of the stairs, and I don't see him, nor do I see the balloon. My children are all that's on my mind; all I want is to see them tucked into the bed made in Grandma's room for the sleepover they so eagerly wanted. Their door is closed, and as I go to open it, there is red in the corner of my eye. The balloon is behind me, floating up towards the 9-ft ceiling. It makes the whole hovering around downstairs that much scarier. Opening the boys' bedroom door, I see them on their foamy's on the floor, safe and sound.

I slowly closed the door, letting out a huge sigh of relief. I turn around, and my mom is behind me with a serious look of concern. "Becca, I know you saw, what I saw! There was someone holding onto that balloon, wasn't there? Why on earth is it high up on your ceiling now stuck up there? It was full of helium, so it's not like it was deflating!"

"I know, Mom, it freaked me out too. This is the kind of weird stuff that happens."

"Let me tell you, Becca, this is beyond weird. Someone pushed me down the stairs earlier and someone wanted us to see him with the balloon today."

Telling my mom I saw the little boy at the top of the stairs and dart into the room around the corner from hers isn't a good idea. She is clearly already alarmed, and I need to calm her down. *I'll tell her in the morning, or better yet, when she leaves.* She needs to get some sleep here.

"Okay... it's late and I'm tired, this day seems to have taken a turn. Let's say goodnight and talk more about this in the morning."

"I'm not going to sleep tonight, Becca."

"Let's try, Mom" We head down the stairs to announce we were going to bed. I left Mitch to turn off the lights, and I head to my room to crawl directly into my bed. My mom upstairs is talking to dad about the red balloon. "I'm sorry, but something's not right," I could hear her say.

Ten minutes later, Mitch is in our bathroom getting ready for bed when my bedroom door flies open, startling me. I see my mom. "What are you doing?" I ask, surprised.

"Becca, I'm so scared to go to bed. The energy is so thick and heavy upstairs I can feel it. I went into our bedroom and the red balloon was there hovering at the end of my bed eye level! So I took it all the way to Logan's room and let it float to the top of the ceiling. I went into the bathroom a minute to brush my teeth. When I went back to our room I saw it floating at the end of our bed in the exact same spot!" My mom is as freaked out as I am, but I just don't want to show it. "Becca, I brushed my teeth for a minute... a minute! And it floated from one end of the house to my room again! I grabbed it and put it in our bedroom closet and closed the door."

"Well, that's good, Mom. It will just stay in there and maybe deflate."

Mitch walks into the room. "Whatcha talking about?" He looks at my mom and me.

"Oh, nothing," Mom says. "I just wanted to say goodnight again." She walks to the door and looks at me one last time, closing it behind her. I'm not going to sleep tonight; she's right about the house. It is vibrating with activity, and having my parents here isn't slowing anything down from happening. If he wants to be seen, he will show himself, and he is.

Hours go by, and I'm letting go of the thoughts of tonight and drifting off into a deep sleep. I had to take melatonin to help me settle, and it's helping my eyelids get heavy. Finally, my mind lets go, and I'm drifting off when a slow squeak of my bedroom's door handle turning disrupts me. My eyes are so heavy, but I try to look and let them adjust to the bedroom door. My bedroom door is wide open. Sitting up, I call out, "Boys? Mom? Who is in my room?" Something is moving at the end of my bed as a dark shadow walking across and turning the corner, coming up my side of the bed. My eyes are continuing to adjust, but the moonlight from the pool gives me just enough light to know what I'm seeing. My heart is starting to race and beating so hard out of my chest. My palms instantly sweat, and pure terror is in the back of my throat as I can only get out the words, "Oh no, oh God no."

It's the blood-red balloon walking its way towards me with a small silhouette and a child's giggle. The shuffling of tiny feet on the carpet is now turning into a fast gallop. The string of the balloon is running towards me, with the red balloon following behind. The dark shadow of the child is running straight at me at full speed. In total panic, I reach for my lamp switch and see it has been removed. I can't turn on the lamp. Knocking it to the ground, I grab my phone and push the flashlight button on the home screen. The light turns on and floods my room with brightness. The balloon stops instantly in its tracks, half a foot from me, then shooting straight up to the top of the high ceiling, where it hit high above my head.

"Becca, why is your flashlight on?" Mitch says groggily.

"I spilled my water, babe, I knocked the lamp over. Sorry, let me clean it up." I head to the bathroom with my legs shaking, feeling like jello; they want to completely give out from under me at any moment. I want to collapse and cry; I want to get sick. What I really want is to move my family out of this horrifying house. Grabbing a towel bringing it to my side of the bed, I clean up the water from the nightstand and pat the wet carpet. The boy is long gone, but his balloon still floats on my ceiling, teasing me. Mitch can't know about this; he is also not a believer of the paranormal, what would he think? It would freak him out still, I'm sure. He works so darn hard; he doesn't need to worry about his own home. While cleaning up my mess, I notice my clock reads 3:39 am. *I can't do this; I can't sleep with that balloon in my room.* The balloon, it's still stuck at the top.

I turn off the flashlight on my phone and head towards the bedroom door, closing it behind me. This isn't the first time I've gotten up after 3 am; for me, insomnia appears every couple of months, but this was different. This was out of fear. After this, sleep is impossible to achieve, and I need to think long and hard about what needs to be done next. This is my home, my safe place, and it feels anything but that at this moment.

Turning the living room lamp on, I hear someone behind me shoveling their feet on my carpet. Startled, I spin around, and my heart takes another sharp pain of panic. It's my mom half asleep. "Becca, my closet and bedroom doors are open."

"I know, Mom."

"What do you mean you know? Were you in my room?"

"No, the boy was. I assume he wanted his balloon." She looks at me speechless and sits on the chair beside me.

I fill her in on what had happened over a cup of tea. We both aren't getting back to sleep. We sit there in silence, just staring at each other, taking all the information in. We hear a door creak upstairs, and we know what room it is. It's Logan's room. We also know it isn't the boys or Dad who just closed it. Staring at each other, not saying a word, we just stay in silence and know.

CHAPTER 7

There's nothing lovely about your body feeling weak and almost hungover from lack of sleep. Your brain doesn't work properly; it's slowly processing, and some things are foggy. Simple conversations or tasks take more concentration, but my mother and I put on our happy faces and push forward. Mitch has taken the boys off to school before his meeting downtown, and my dad has left for the clubhouse to work out, leaving my mom and me to discuss what the next plan is.

"Becca, I think there has to be a record of an accident or something?"

"Mom, the realtor said there was nothing, but I'll check again with you."

We spent an hour trying to find anything on our address, and not one thing comes up. Thankfully, the house has been quiet this morning, and I'm relieved. My heart can't handle more scares. I've been feeling sharp pains in my chest, and I'm sure it's from the stress. The red balloon is now floating above the front door and almost looks stuck at the windowsill. No one would be able to reach it unless they had a tall ladder. *I can't wait until it deflates.* Logan's balloon is still attached to a chair off of the living room. The boys aren't playing with it and won't miss it at all, especially me. I am popping the balloon, removing it from the chair, and stuffing it deep in the garbage can. I do not want a replay of last night's occurrences ever again. My mom closes my computer defeated; our search brings up not one thing on this house; it's a dead-end with no answers.

"I don't know, Mom, there clearly is someone in this house, maybe it's time I bring Mitch up to speed."

"Do that after we leave in a couple days, it will be less pressure for him to accept and just the two of you."

I nod. It's a good idea and gives me enough time to figure out how to do this. The front door opens, and Dad walks in. "That gym is great. I even showered down there. It's like a spa." I laugh. I'm glad he's enjoying a normal vacation, what I would do for a normal house.

"Glad you enjoyed it. Shall we head out for lunch before we grab the kids from school?"

"Great idea," Mom says. "I'll grab my things." She gives me a reassuring smile, rubs my back, and walks up the stairs. I'm so glad she can see what's going on in the house; I'm not alone, and I'm not crazy.

I head over to my room and change into a nice summer dress. Right before I open my bedroom door to leave, I stop and talk out loud, "You know, I don't know who you are or what you want, but this isn't funny, and this is my home and family. It's time you move on and leave us alone. You're not welcome here." Standing there in silence, not sure what to expect next. No response, and I'm grateful for that; it's worth a shot. I grab my things and head out. Maybe that's all he needed to hear, but I somehow think that's not the case.

A few hours go by, and we get back with the kids; Mitch walks a couple of hours later from what looks like a very successful day at work. He has a little pep to his step, and there's no way I'm going to bring up anything that may put a cloud over his mood.

"Let's open some wine tonight," Mitch says, "I just got a great promotion at work today and we need to celebrate."

"That's great, babe!" I lean in for a kiss.

"It means I will have to do some more traveling, but it will be completely worth it."

"Congratulations, Mitch!" my dad says.

It's sad that the first thing I think about is *I'm going to be alone with the kids in this house.* Shaking my head, I snap myself out of it, putting on a supportive smile. I'm not going to think like that now; we are celebrating tonight. He deserves this moment. We have some dinner; afterward, I read a new book to the kids while tucking them into bed. Spending the evening by the pool while watching the sunset and the skies turn into cotton candy colors; brings relaxation and a breath of fresh air. Dusk finally arrives, and Mitch turns the pool lights on, then comes over to light the outdoor fireplace. *This is heaven*, I think to myself while taking it all in. This moment makes me love this house so much, it's our home, and it is so beautiful. The night insects start singing their tune, and I walk over to the remote and turn the hot tub on.

"I'm going to have a soak; anyone want to join?"

"I will," my mom says, "I'm going to go get changed and check in on the boys!"

"Okay!" I nod. I pour us some red wine by the hot tub and look up at the sky. It's dark now, and her room light turns on; it looks over the pool. There are jet black clouds in the far distance, and I know a storm is rolling in. Nothing beats a good Texas storm, but it could turn bad, including close encounters with tornados. However, I do know what to do and what to expect if one rolls in fast. My mom's room light switches off, and shortly after, she's stepping outside in her bathing suit. She comes over to the tub, and we step in, letting out a sign of pure relaxation and exhaustion. The hot tub heats up so fast, and the hum of the jets just melts all thoughts away.

"Are the boys still good?" I ask.

"Oh yes, fast asleep. I closed their door and got changed as quickly as I could in the bathroom. I just hate being upstairs alone. At least your dad sleeps well, in fact being here has given him the best sleep he's had in months."

"That's good," I reply. We hear the crackle of the storm in the distance, and the sky lights up.

"We have a bad one coming soon," says Mitch looking at his weather app on his phone.

"Under another tornado warning, should be here in an hour."

"A couple more minutes and we will wrap it up and tuck everything away," I say. It's almost pitch black outside, with just the patio light and the outdoor fireplace letting off a warm glow. "Mom, we should get out and get ready for the storm. We may need to move you all down to the first floor depending on the severity of it."

"Good idea, I don't want to become Dorothy." We all laugh and start to step out of the tub, drying ourselves off, when suddenly we hear a loud snap. We find ourselves in complete darkness. All of the outdoor patio lights turn off, along with every light left on, inside the house. We freeze, waiting for some light to guide us.

"What just happened?" my mom asks.

My dad is faintly illuminated by the outdoor fireplace that is still on. It's the only source of light anywhere. He stands up. "Is this a power outage?"

Mitch steps out, "I guess! The storm is still far enough away that you would think we wouldn't be affected yet. Who knows." Mitch shrugs. "I know where some flashlights are." Mitch heads inside.

"Mom, it's dark." A chilly breeze blows past me, causing chills to run down my spine. I get an eerie feeling that someone's watching me, that feeling that something is just not right.

"Becca?" Mom says as she stares towards the house.

"What?" I say, looking at her, following the direction of her eyes.

The lightning flashed in the sky, startling us. As soon as the flash was over, the lights in the house turn on for a split second. Then, the lights start to flicker on and off. There, in my mother's room, we see the boy standing at the window with both hands placed on the glass, looking down at us with a smile —a smile of unimaginable pure evil.

"Becca!" Mom screams and pushes past me.

In the darkness, I stumble on the steps of the hot tub, knocking over the wine glasses, and hear them shattering on the concrete. We both run towards the house. My feet miss the last step down from the hot tub landing, and I fall hard to the ground. When I look back up at the window, the lights flash back on in the house. The little boy is watching us while we frantically make our way to the house. Right at that moment, my mom runs past my dad at full speed. She gets to the open back door right as it slams shut with such force throwing her back on the ground three feet away from the door.

"Mom!" I shriek. Picking myself up, I can feel my knees badly lacerated with the sensation of warm blood running down my cut-up legs. My dad flies off his chair to help my mom lying on the ground, holding her face.

"What the hell was that? Are you okay?" My dad asks my mom as she is still on the ground screaming in agony.

Mitch comes out. "Was that the door? What happened?" He heads over to my parents, and all I can think is the kids and that boy upstairs! I hobble past them into the house running through the living room and to the bottom of the stairs. The pain in my leg is excruciating, but it doesn't slow me down as adrenaline kicks in. My hand is on the railings, and I launch myself up the stairs. A child's laughter is echoing from everywhere on the second floor. The bedroom door to my right slams shut. Taking no notice bolting towards the room my children are in, thrusting open the door. Standing at the door, I look down to see them sleeping undisturbed and unaware of the drama occurring. My legs give out, and my body collapses by the bed in relief. With a slight whimper, I hold back the tears I want to let out. I think *I can't bear this feeling any longer.* Pulling myself up, I bend over and pick up the sleeping Logan. Then, I softly wake Connor up as well.

"Mommm? What's going on?" Connor asks.

"Baby, a storm is coming, and I thought it would be fun to have a sleepover in Mommy's room." I'm not leaving my kids alone for a single second tonight. We make our way downstairs, and Mitch walks in from outside.

"What are you doing? What's all this blood?" Looking down, I see bloody footprints everywhere. I must have really cut up my feet from the wine glasses when they shattered. "I'll take the kids and put them in our room, you get your dad to check on your feet."

I don't even know where to start. Grabbing a towel, I hobble outside to see my mom sitting in a chair with my dad kneeling beside her. "Mom!" I say, clearly shaken.

"The kids?" She asks.

"They are fine. I grabbed them and Mitch is setting them up a bed in our room." My mom is holding a blood-soaked towel up to her face.

"I think she just hit her face hard on the door, her nose doesn't look broken. Thank God," my father explains in relief. "I'll get a fresh towel and some ice." My dad heads back into the house.

"Mom!" It's all I could get out.

"I know, Becca, I saw him too. He slammed that door so hard it could have killed me. There's no wind, the storm is still coming but miles away."

"I know!" Hot tears start running down my face. "Mom, I'm so sorry."

"Becca, this isn't your fault, but you have to get out of this house. It's not safe."

Dad comes out with a first aid kit and a new towel for Mom. "Becca, let's see your feet." He starts picking out glass shards touching the open cuts; I wince in pain. Then, looking up at the sky, the storm is about to show its ugly head soon. Lightning casts light upon the pool, followed by a loud crack when something catches my eye near the hot tub. There are the wine glasses that had been knocked over and broken on the ground, along with my blood, which had pooled around the glass. But there is something else. My eyes glaze over with tears, tears of terror and defeat. The bloody marks by the hot tub are shaped like child's feet. Footprints stamped in my own blood that look as if a child was dancing—dancing in my own blood around and around. The color drains from my face; everything gets foggy and then black.

CHAPTER 8

My memory is hazy the next morning. Completely
overwhelmed, hoping it was all just a dream or, even better,
more like a nightmare. My feet and knees are all bandaged up
from being badly cut but thankfully didn't need any stitches.
My mom has a huge cut on her nose; it's starting to take the
shape of a bad bruise and possibly black eyes to go with. My
parents leave tomorrow morning, and my anxiety has kicked
into overdrive as I start to think of what's to come.

They're packing their bags, and all I want to do is beg them
to stay. I know this is something I have to figure out on my
own, but I don't want to. Every time the house has a big night
of unexplained paranormal activity, it always goes rather quiet
for a couple of days. Almost as if it ran out of energy from the
night before. The boy makes no appearances; no doors slam
shut or early morning visits in my bedroom. It's the only time I
get any rest and really think of what the hell am I to do.

My mom and I go outside to enjoy the peace and quiet
before the boys come home from school excited for the
weekend. "Becca, I'm serious now. I really don't think it's a
good idea for you to stay in this house. With all that's gone
wrong with it and what we've seen, I think it's time to find
something else."

"I know, Mom, but I just can't get up and move again. That's all we do, and we have just gotten settled. Plus, what the heck am I going to tell Mitch? Babe we need to move because there's a little unknown boy in this house who I have seen from the very first day?"

"Yes," she replies. "Start there."

My mouth is closed; she's right, but I just can't. The front door swings open, and in comes the circus of madness as the boys run right for Grandma. Living so far away from family is hard, especially when in need of them more than ever. We enjoy a nice family dinner together and head to bed early, knowing their flight leaves first thing in the morning. We say our goodnights, and I head to the room to snuggle right in and fall into a deep slumber right away. Days of little to no sleep have finally caught up, and my body couldn't take another second of being awake. Hours later, I roll over to see the alarm clock read 3:39 AM. I'm not even going to look around our bedroom. Rolling over right up to the back of Mitch, feeling his warmth on my body, holding him tight, and keeping my eyes closed. Not tonight.

***

My parents left a couple of days ago, and Mitch is now packing his suitcase for his business trip.

"I'm going to be gone for just three days, but I set up the video surveillance I bought at Costco. Man is that thing cool. Just look at the app I installed on your phone and you have a perfect view of the front and back yard 24-7."

"Yes, Mitch." I roll my eyes. "I will be fine. We live in the safest community in Dallas and my girlfriends are right next door." However, I'm worried about the inside of the house, not the outside.

"Give me a kiss and I'll hit the road." He grabs my waist and pulls me towards him. I let out a giggle, and our lips meet. The love radiates from his kiss, but it breaks my heart that I'm not telling him everything.

"Got to run." He winks, and just like that, he's out the door. I stand in the same spot and sigh. *This should be interesting!* Grabbing the keys, I head to the front door. Spending the least amount of time as possible in this house alone is what I need to do.

Later that day, we get home from a Mommy and sons' dinner date at the new Italian restaurant not far away.

"That was good Mom, I'm so full I love spaghetti! Like really love it!"

"It was good, Connor." I smile. "Now let's go for a nice swim before unwinding for bed."

"Great idea, Mom!" Connor yells, running upstairs to his room to get changed.

Just like that, every single door in the house slams shut simultaneously with such force it knocked off family photos on every wall. My heart jumped out of my chest and Logan, who was in my arms, immediately starts crying from the noise.

"Connor!" I scream, running up the stairs.

"Mom, I'm okay," he says as he was standing in the hallway outside of his room.

"Mom, what happened?"

"I don't know baby, maybe the windows are open and the wind just shut the doors. It happens sometimes." I know damn well that is not the case. All the windows are closed and the air conditioner on. All doors slammed at the exact same second. How is that even possible? I open his bedroom door. "There we go, let's get you changed and go swimming."

Getting him changed, I hustle Connor along down the stairs and outside. He dives straight into the pool while my nerves start to settle.

"I have a great idea. Who wants to do a fun sleepover in my room tonight?"

"Yes, Mom! Me! Can we all make a tent and camp like we do at Grandma's?"

"Yes," I reply. Keeping my babies close until Mitch is home is my priority. I can almost feel the energy of the house increasing daily and building like it's a static charge. My cell phone rings, and sleeping Logan jumps high in my arms. "Sorry baby, go back to sleep."

"Hello?"

"Hi babe, how's the pool?"

"The pool? How do y…" I look up at the blinking camera and smile, letting out a cheeky wave.

"Man, this thing is cool. I feel like I won't miss a thing. I can see Connor's cannonball from here."

I laugh. "Yes, he does that well, how was the drive?"

"Good," he responds, "I'm bagged but I have a huge presentation due tomorrow, so I have at least another couple hours of work before I hit the sack."

"Awe, hun, that's no good. At least you're there."

"Yeah I just wanted to check in. Have a good night and kiss the boys for me. I'll call you tomorrow."

"Sounds good, love you." Just like that, I'm on my own again.

"Connor, it's time to get out of the pool it's time for a bath and jammies."

I'm lucky; my little boy rarely gives me a hard time. This is why we wanted another child, and now I feel complete with my two boys. After we make a quick tent in our room out of our king sheets, making a rather comfy bed on the floor. Logan is now lying down, and he's not even aware of his surroundings; he's in a deep sleep.

"Let's be quiet because Logan's sleeping, but let's read a story of your choice."

"This one, Mom." Connor picks up another one of his favorites, the cartoon book Star Wars, a new hope.

"Of course!" I look over and smile. We have only read this a million times, and I can read it a million more. Finishing the book, we snuggle down under the covers with Connor now fast asleep. I hope he remembers these precious moments of tents and sleepovers because I will. Slowly, my eyes start closing, and I think—doors locked-check, windows closed-check, alarm on-check, video surveillance on-check. I'm okay to sleep, and off I drifted.

Waking up a couple of hours later, I open my eyes slowly. I've been lying on my side with my back to the kids, and now my left arm is asleep and tingling. The floors are just not as comfy as you get older, no matter how much foam you put down—rolling off my arm now laying on my back staring up at the tent sheets. I glance over and see Connor snoring while Logan's sleeping like a starfish with his hand across Connor's face. "These boys!" I chuckle.

At this moment, a clicking sound from the far corner of my room catches my attention. Turning my head, I have the perfect view of under my bed. The sound was familiar; it's the sound of my bedroom door. Watching the door from under my bed, I see it slowly opening. "Oh God, no!" I whisper. I face my nightstand, and now my line of sight is covered from all these sheets over us. My breathing is increasing, and my heart is starting to race again.

I stare at the bottom of the door, praying that's it, let this be everything that happens tonight—closing my eyes, ignoring everything completely. Just then, the sound of movement from the doorway grabs my attention. As I'm turning my head out of the darkness, two pale feet step in. "This isn't happening, please, please!" I'm pleading for this madness to stop. My eyes stare at the small white, pale feet and bony ankles in my doorway and watch him start to take his first steps entering my bedroom. He is coming around to the bottom of my bed, shuffling with each step. Now I can't see him because of the tent we made; he is out of my view completely, the damn sheets are in the way. *Oh, God, my kids!*

Rolling over, I huddle closer to the boys, whispering a quiet prayer. Glancing up, I start to see a small hand placing its palm and fingers above me on the white sheets, just barely visible with the light of the moon from the window. His little fingers start gripping the sheets above me, and in a split second, they rip from above, flying to the other side of the bedroom. Letting out a terrifying shriek, I then fumble for my nightstand. Turning on the lamp by the pull-string that I had replaces earlier, sending the light flooding the room not leaving a shadow in sight.

Connor sits up, rubbing his eyes. "Mom?"

"It's okay, Connor," "Mom just knocked the sheets off our tent and it scared me."

"Why would you do that?" He asks, annoyed.

"It was an accident baby, go back to sleep." He puts his head back down, and I start to scan around the room. There's no sign of the boy, but the sheets are by the bedroom door.

"That's enough!" I say, hoping this boy can hear me. I'm now sweating in fear and panic every single night of my life. This isn't a game. "This is ridiculous," I utter. While getting up, I move from the doorway and close the master door, making sure to turn the knob and locking it.

Walking into the master bath to wash my face with some ice-cold water will pull myself together. I pat my face dry and look up in the mirror, expecting him to show his face behind me and nothing. Turning off the bathroom light, I make my way out of the bathroom to stop abruptly in my tracks. The sheets lying on a heap by the bedroom door start moving like something is stuck in them. Frozen in my tracks, I now watch them start to take shape, getting taller and taller until they morph into a shape-like-a-child. My whole body feels ill, standing there in shock, not wanting to believe what's right in front of me.

"Mom?" Connor says, pointing at the sheets replicating a child. "Who's that?" Just like that, the head turns towards Connor and disintegrates, letting the sheet fall to the ground on the floor.

"Connor!" I walk past the pile and over to him, giving him a huge hug.

"Mom, that was a neat trick, how did you do that?"

How do I explain this? "I don't know, Connor. I guess some Mommy magic!" I keep the lights on for the remainder of the night, watching over everyone as they sleep. The sheets are now evicted from my room and left in the hallway with the door shut tight behind it. Sleep won't happen tonight; my children need my protection from whatever this is. It's my duty as their mother to keep them safe and not let them witness the unnatural things occurring in this house. I'm to act like their filter and willing to do whatever it takes to shelter them, keeping them protected. This is traumatizing for an adult, let alone a small child.

The sun rises and brings another day. Sometimes when the sun would rise in Dallas, it would be the most majestic sight anyone could ever wish to see. For me, it brings relief; I survived another night. The boys wake up from slumber and run out of the bedroom to play. My feet go straight for the coffee maker; this will be once again a multi-cup-of-java kind of day.

The boys are laughing so hard upstairs it brings a tired smile to my face.

"What's so funny?" I yell up.

"Mom come and see this, when did you do it?"

"Do what?" I say as my voice cuts out. Walking up the stairs briskly, I can see the boys at the top of the landing sitting cross-legged on the floor. Right in front of them are every single Hot Wheels car they own, making a bumper-to-bumper trail all the way to Logan's room. I follow the trail of cars into his room, I gasp. The Hot Wheels cars are in a perfectly shaped spiral going around and around, getting smaller with each lap until it ends right in the center. There, in the center of the trail, is a rusty old truck.

"Mom! Look, I got a new truck!"

"Connor that's not yours, I don't know whose it is, or where it came from." I make a sweeping motion with my feet and drag all the Hot Wheels to the center and start scooping them up with my hand.

"Mom, you are ruining it, it was so cool!".

I clean up every little toy and take the rusty old truck downstairs, marching right to the trash can and toss the rusty truck away. *My children will not be playing with that wherever it came from; thank you.* After things settled down and the kids forgave me for destroying the unknown carpet creation of cars, I put on a movie to buy me some uninterrupted time. I head to the kitchen with the phone in my hand, where there is still a line of sight, but they wouldn't hear me talking.

"Mom, it was like the boy was playing with my kids. He was playing with their toys. How on earth can I explain all of this?" I whisper into the phone. "Last thing I need is Connor getting whiff of this and become completely terrified."

"I don't know, Becca," my mom replies. "Between the sounds of last night and today I really think you should head to a hotel."

"No, I can't do that. Mitch is back in a couple days. I'm just going to bring him up to speed on this house once he is back and hope he believes me."

"Becca, I know he will, maybe he's seen or felt something?".

"You're right, Mom, thanks." I needed to hear this.

85

Ending the conversation, I hang up the phone, wondering

Will he? Will he believe in all of this?

I honestly don't know.

CHAPTER 9

Night creeps up so fast nowadays. I wonder if it senses my anxiety the second the sun sets. The strange daytime occurrences aren't so horrible, but the evening ones scare me to death. The boys are all snuggled in my big bed. Sleepover it is, and I was almost relieved when Conner begged to sleep in our bed. Snuggled in and down for the night, I watch them sleep, looking so peaceful and worry-free. *If only I could sleep like that.*

A couple of hours go by, and I've now finished my book. It's so easy for me to get lost in a good page-turner and almost feel like I'm a part of the novel. *If my current life wasn't a page-turner, maybe I could get some sleep.* Placing the book on my nightstand, I do one last scan of the room before turning off the lamp. It's been a rather quiet house tonight; if only it can stay like this until dawn. My head is now on the cool pillow, and a sigh of fatigue escapes me. It's so much easier with Mitch home. I feel protected.

As I am drifting off to sleep, not soon after, I am awakened by a light on my nightstand. My cell phone next to me is glowing with notifications alerts. I sit up and turn the lamp on. Maybe it's a text from Mitch. Oddly, it is a little late for him.

Reading the alert across the top of my phone: Motion detected at 12:24 AM Camera B.

What? I think to myself. *Maybe an animal in the backyard?* Unlocking the phone with my fingerprint takes me right to the recent notification recording, telling me it was 10 seconds long. As I push the play button, the view of my yard appears with half of the pool and back door. Nothing is moving, and right when I'm about to close the app, there goes Logan's soccer ball flying into a frame. I bring my phone closer to my face. It's not windy out. Is someone in my backyard?

My finger scrolls down to the live feed option, and I click. The loading wheel goes around and around. The camera goes straight to night vision. My stomach drops, and I let out a terrifying gasp as the live feed finishes loading on my phone. There, right front and center, is the little boy, standing right in the middle of the camera feed looking straight up at the camera motionless. Letting out a whimper, my phone drops in my lap as I bring my hands to cover the sounds that were pouring out of my mouth—not wanting to wake the boys, muffling the terror that was escaping. Looking down at my phone, I pick it back up. The little boy is still standing there staring up; he isn't even blinking. He is so pale wearing dark pants and an old t-shirt. Something doesn't look right. I look closely and see his eyes have no pupil; they are just pure black.

The pale boy slowly starts to grin again with his pale chapped lips showing small rotten teeth with his smile, then he turns around and starts walking towards the pool, walking out of frame. I hear a huge splash outside from my master window and throw the covers from my body, heading right to the window to peer out. Pushing apart the blinds, I can see the pool water is settling from a disturbance; there are watermarks on the concrete beside the pool. My eyes feel strained as they're trying so hard to adjust, as I'm searching and looking around for the boy in the darkness of my yard. Just like that, a wet juvenile handprint slams the other side of the window by my face, and I watch the moisture drizzle down from the mark he left. Immediately closing the blinds, I take a couple of steps back from the window. *This is not happening.* I feel dizzy again.

Rushing over to my phone, I attempt to dial Mitch as fast as I can. It tries to connect, ringing and ringing. "Come on Mitch, answer!"

"Hello?" Mitch answers groggily.

"Mitch! Mitch! Someone is in our backyard!"

"What? Wait, are you sure?"

"Yes, I'm sure, why do you think I'm calling?"

"What happened? Let me take a look," he says.

"Listen, there was a motion notification recorded and then a boy was standing by the camera and then someone jumped in our pool!"

"Hang on, hang on, are you okay? Are the boys okay?" he asks, alarmed.

"Yes, they are fast asleep and I'm in the house, the alarms on."

"I can see the recording of the ball, but I don't see a boy or anyone else. Where is that recording?"

I'm so frazzled I stop to think. "That was the live feed."

"Becca calm down. If there was a boy or any kids in the backyard that came up on the live feed it would have also been picked up as movement and recorded... right?"

"Well... yes but—"

"No but... it's okay, you probably saw some fog or mist on the camera. I'm checking all the feeds and there is nothing or no one on our property. It could have been an animal that stumbled on the ball in the feed. Maybe it was the damn rats or a raccoon." He chuckles.

"Mitch, it wasn't an animal, this isn't funny. I heard someone jump in our pool. There were even water marks." I haven't even told Mitch about the wet handprint on the window yet, and it already isn't going very well. I can hear the doubt in his voice.

"Everything is alright, babe, I'll add some locks to our side gates in case some neighborhood teens wanted to go for an evening dip. You remember how it was being a teen, the thrill of almost getting caught doing something that makes your heart jump?"

"No!" I said, "I never did stupid stuff like that, maybe it was nothing. I'm sorry I woke you."

"Don't ever be sorry, Becca, I'm home tomorrow. Are you going to be okay?" Mitch asks.

"Yes," I reply. "I'm good, goodnight and see you tomorrow."

"Night, love you," he says, and the phone call ends.

Sitting there holding the phone in my hand, I look over towards the windows. I know what I saw; I know it was the same boy. Perhaps he thinks this is a playful game, but this crap is getting old. I lay back and leave my lamp on. *I think I'm going to start another book tonight; clearly, sleep isn't forecasted for me yet again.*

CHAPTER 10

Mitch comes home to a quiet house, but not the kids being quiet, the lack of supernatural energy. The house has gone entirely dormant with no unexplainable activity. Days go by, and still nothing. There hasn't been an opportunity to talk to Mitch and let him know what really has been going on in this house. I know that I must have the conversation with him, but avoiding it for this long has left it rather uncomfortable. I never keep anything from Mitch, but it's about time.

"Mitch, let's have a glass of wine by the pool," Passing him a glass of cabernet.

"Baby, you read my mind." He smiles. "Hot tub?"

"Sure, maybe after." We walk out the backdoor and sit down on the outdoor wicker loveseat. "I've been meaning to talk to you about something, and don't really know where to start."

"At the beginning is usually the best start." He snickers.

"Since the very first day I stepped into this house odd things have been happening. When we moved in I started to see them more. Like the night I hurt your back, for example."

"Okay," he says. I can feel his hesitation. "Like what?"

"I have been seeing a young boy in this house. Sometimes in our room, at windows and the other night I told you someone was on the live backyard feed from our camera. I think this place has some sort of spirit."

Mitch frowns and looks at me. "Like it's haunted?"

"Yes, Mitch. I think this house is haunted by a child, it's the same boy I've seen from the window the day we first drove away."

"What! You never told me this before." Mitch snaps.

"I didn't because I wasn't sure. I'm sure now. Something has been going on and it's getting worse."

Mitch lifts his hand and touches the side of my face pulling my hair behind my ear. "Becca, this is the silliest thing I have ever heard and really think you should lay off the scary movies and books you read. I don't believe in ghosts and think this is all ridiculous. Everything can have a logical explanation."

I knew it; I knew he would never believe me.

"We have been here for almost half a year and not once have I seen anything unexplainable, definitely no ghost child."

"What are you talking about, Mitch? When my mom was here the lights powered off and all doors slammed with great force throwing her back 7 feet, remember?".

"Explainable. It's called a storm. Windows and doors left open created an airflow disturbance. I really don't want to talk about this anymore. I would much rather spend some alone time with you. How about you and I have a date night in the tub right now, just the two of us?" Mitch stands up and grabs my hand pulling me up off the loveseat. He smiles, moving in for a kiss. "Now no more of this talk, let's have a good night. Meet you in the tub." Mitch walks into the house to get changed. I'm left standing outside with the cool summer breeze. "Well, that's that," I say to myself, feeling defeated. Now I know I'm really on my own.

***

Days go by, and nothing changes. The house hasn't started buzzing with energy, and Mitch has been home the entire time, so sleeping has been a bit better. Our kids were over at the neighbor's house playing one afternoon, and I had the entire house to myself. Mitch was out running errands, and I decided to take a really good look around the house. Maybe something would happen, or maybe I would find a secret door or something in the attic. Who knows at this point. The attic is where I start, and it's so hot from the Texas sun pounding on the roof, climbing the latter further, walking around the hot water tank. It was always strange to me to have hot water tanks in attics, but they don't have basements in Texas, so it makes sense. Nothing jumps out at me.

Climbing down the stairs, sweating from the heat, I push the retractable ladder back up, closing the ceiling door, now making my way to the stairs. Suddenly, from the corner of my eye, something runs fast from Logan's room, catching my attention.

"Hello?" I call out. Of course, nothing replies, but I know I'm not alone. "Listen, I don't have a problem with you here as long as you don't do any scary stuff to me or my children." I feel so stupid saying this, but hey, I will try anything at this point.

The doorbell rings downstairs and breaks up the eerie moment. Heading downstairs, making my way to the front door. "Mommmmm!" The boys bust past me.

"Hi, Becca," says Carol. We ladies have grown so much closer over the last couple of months, and it has been a relief to have someone in your corner when family doesn't live close.

"Hi Carol, want to come in?"

"Oh no, I just brought the boys over because I'm dropping my kids off at the in-laws' house for the weekend. I think they were all mad I cut their playtime short." She laughs.

"I hear ya."

"I was thinking of getting some girls together and head to the Vin Room for a couple glasses of wine tonight. They have a live band inside too!" The Vine Room is a swanky new restaurant that recently opened up catered more to extensive wine selections. I have always wanted to check it out in person.

"You know, Carol, that sounds perfect."

"Great, I will pick you up out front at 8 pm," Carol says with a smile.

" Looking forward to it." Closing the door, I can honestly say I'm looking forward to this night out with some ladies and thinking about something other than this house.

Like clockwork, Carol is in her driveway waiting for me at eight on the dot. Both of us dressed in nice summer dresses; we can't help but feel a little giddy with excitement; we looked good. "I love leaving the husband with the kids," she says as we drive off. "This way he gets a good taste of playing, bath, story-time, and then the kids not going to bed." She laughs.

"Mine are already in bed so Mitch is lucky," I say.

We pull up to the Vin Room four minutes later. It had opened up right outside our community gates, so it was definitely convenient. We walk into this busy little establishment, and I'm in awe of the huge wall of floor-to-ceiling wine bottles. Every single bottle you can imagine. The place is stunning.

"Becca, we have a spot on the patio. I can see the ladies." We walk out the back doors, and it takes us to the outdoor oasis of luxurious outdoor seating with oversized chairs, pillows, and stunning outdoor fireplaces, all bringing such an ambiance to the patio.

"Wow, this is nice." Looking around in complete awe. We walk up to a group of ladies who are waving us over with eager smiles.

"Isn't it?" says Carol. "Ladies, this is Becca, my neighbor I was telling you about."

"Becca, so nice to meet you, my name is Faith." One of the ladies gets up and hugs me.

"Oh," I say. I'm caught off guard with such a big strong embrace right out the front door.

"We hug here." She laughs. "All the time, plus a friend of Carol's is a friend of ours. Have a seat." Faith pats the spot right next to her. I sit down and sink into the comfiest outdoor couch I have ever sat in.

"Hi, I'm Sarah," says the last lady sitting next to Carol.

"Nice to meet you all," I say, feeling my face getting red with all the attention on me, the new girl.

"Let's order some bottles, you choose one, Becca," says Carol. "Sarah, you too."

"Oh, I will Carol. This mommy has no kids for a couple days because they are out camping with Daddy. I definitely will be enjoying a bottle or two." She looks at me with a wink. "Mitch and I really enjoy the Castello Banfi Brunello!"

"Great taste! Made in Tuscany, Italy. I spent last summer there. Completely breathtaking."

"Let's order a 2009 Marcassin Chardonnay and some appetizers for our palates." The young male waiter walks up to our area and takes our order. It doesn't take long for wine to start flowing while the band inside kicks off. I'm glad we are sitting outside so we can hear each other over the roaring band. As time goes by, I start to enjoy myself.

"So, Becca, we've talked about husbands, kids… tell us something else. How do you like the area?"

I start to loosen up and really feel a connection with the ladies. It's fun. "I love it here, everyone is so nice. It's warm almost all the time which is a bonus since I'm from Canada."

"How do you like the house?" Sarah asks. All ladies stop and stare at me.

I swallow a huge mouthful of wine and can feel its effects on my body. "It's nice."

"Nice?" Faith asks. "That's all? Tell us more about it."

They must know it's haunted. They continue to stare at me, waiting to give them some dirt. Do they know something about my house? "It's a good little house, but has had some bad luck. You know the lack of copper when we moved in, no lines, the rodents, and the disappearing pool equipment. I kinda think there's something else too." I let out a nervous giggle.

Should I continue or stop right here? I don't need new friends to think I'm off my rocker with a childish ghost story.

"Something else like what?" asks Faith.

"I swear I keep seeing a young child, a boy."

All of a sudden, a smash abruptly stops the conversation. Sarah's wine glass hit the floor and shatters by her feet. "Oh God, I'm so sorry," she says as she reaches for a napkin and dabs the ground of red wine and glass shards.

We all get up to help her, but the waiter is already coming over with a broom and dustpan.

"Sorry, I think I've had too much wine. Can I get some water please?" She asks the waiter.

"Sure," he replies as he walks away with a pan full of sharp glass. While he walks away, I notice all the ladies looking back at me. They clearly want me to continue my story.

"It's weird but strange things have been happening since we moved in and I honestly can't explain it."

Sarah abruptly stands up. "I'm sorry guys, I can't sit here and listen to this. Someone needs to tell her and it's not going to be me. It was nice meeting you. Becca. Ladies." She nods at the other two.

"Sarah, what? Wait! This is silly, come here." Carol is already chasing Sarah through the patio doors, and I'm left stunned.

What just happened?

"Becca, I'm so sorry. Clearly Sarah has had too much to drink," Faith says as she scoots next to me.

"What the hell did she mean?' Tell me what?" I snap. "Why is everything so secretive when it comes to my house? Everyone is always curious. Why?" Just then, my phone rings and breaks up the awkward moment between Faith and me.

"Hello?"

"Hey babe, how's it going?" It's Mitch, and it's kind of strange he's calling just a couple of hours into a girls' night.

"Are the kids okay?" I ask.

"Yes, sleeping. They were playing a game on me and running around upstairs after I tucked them in. They were setting the musical night light in Logan's room and a couple of his loud fire trucks. By the time I got upstairs, they ran into the room and pretended to sleep."

"Pretended?"

"Yeah, I think so. It was weird." Mitch laughs. It wasn't a regular Mitch laugh; it was forced. He needs me. Without a doubt, I bet he's creeped out since I shared my concerns about the house with him.

"I'm finishing up here and coming home now. See you soon." I hang up without hearing his response and stand up. It is time to go; this night turned sour fast, and sitting here any longer wouldn't make sense. "Faith, it was nice meeting you but I have to run home."

"Not you too," she says.

"Yes, I have to. Tell Carol I say goodbye and I'll talk to her tomorrow."

Faith stands up for a hug and gives me a sad face as if it would guilt trip me into staying for another glass. It is not happening. Grabbing my purse, I pay my bill at the counter inside. Carol is walking back in with no Sarah, so I b-line it out the door right into a waiting cab. I was done socializing and needed to get home.

The cab pulls up in front of my house minutes later; paying him, I open the door to step out. My eyes are immediately diverted, looking up at Logan's room where the lights are flickering on and off so fast, similar to a strobe light. The cab driver, who has his window down, looks up at the lights flickering and says, "Party?" with a chuckle. Looking at Logan's window, I respond, "Yeah, something like that".

When I walk into the house, Mitch is standing in the kitchen. "Babe, you didn't need to come home, I got this."

"I know," I responded and walking over to him, putting my purse on the counter. "I'm tired and wanted to finish my night off with you at home." He leans in for a long kiss and chuckles.

"Brunello, huh?"

I laugh. "Yes".

"Let's head to bed," Mitch says while leading me towards our room.

"Give me one second, I want to check on the kids." Breaking away, I head towards the stairs.

"Okay, set the alarm, will you?" Mitch heads down the hall.

Climbing the stairs quietly, I'm almost straining to hear any sound; nothing. I get to the top of the stairs and can see Logan's room. The lights have calmed down, and the room is dark, almost sleeping. Making my way towards Connor's room, placing my hand on the doorknob, turning it ever so slowly. Peering in, they're fast asleep. The room is lit with the bright full moon outside. *The blinds must be open.* I open the door enough to see the window. The blinds are wide open, and right in front of it is a silhouette of a small boy standing facing the door, looking right at me. Letting out a gasp, I fumble frantically for the light switch.

Finally, I find it, and the lights come on, and the silhouette disappears with the brightness of the room. It's gone; no one is standing in the room. My heart races as I take a breath, trying to slow it down. The light doesn't affect the quality of the kids' slumber, thank goodness. I look one more time around the room for the boy and see nothing. Relieved, I turn the light off and wait for my eyes to adjust. Still nothing; he was gone.

"Leave them alone," I whisper. I must've stood upstairs standing in their room for what felt like hours, making sure he never came back. He was gone. This is ridiculous, and maybe I saw something else after a good bottle of wine. I head towards the stairs and glance around—nothing up here. I descended the stairs, then headed to the front door to set the alarm. As I punched in our passcode, the alarm made a sound letting me know it is armed and the house is now secure. I turn off the lights and walk to the master bedroom. The sensation of someone watching me is still there, and I'm fighting the urge to turn around and look—goodnight.

***

A few hours later, I'm suddenly awoken and sitting straight up to our house alarm blaring.

"What's that? Our alarm?" Mitch yells.

"Yes!" I yell back. I pull the covers back instantly. A mother's first instinct is her babies; they are down the hall and upstairs, which in moments like these seems so far away. Mitch grabs a bat he had under the bed and heads for our master door. Without even thinking, I push past him and run into the darkness. I glance around the living room and run for the stairs straight for the kids.

"Becca! Wait!" Mitch yells. By the time he screamed for me to wait, I'm already up the stairs and at Connor's closed door, pushing it open.

"Mom? What's that sound?" The boys are both sitting up in bed, holding their hands over their ears.

"It's nothing, my love, Daddy accidentally set off the alarm, silly Dad." I smile, hoping the boys mirror my face reassuring them that everything is okay.

Mitch is trying to punch in the code to deactivate the alarm, and it's not taking. "Becca! I can't turn this dam thing off."

"Mom will be right back." Heading out their bedroom door, I hear the boys laughing, thinking this is rather a funny debacle. My mind is so flustered that I cannot even think with all the blaring noise. I head down the stairs holding the railing, with my legs shaking with adrenaline. Finally, after two attempts, the alarm takes, and the loud siren has now stopped.

"That had to have woken up the whole street," Mitch says. "I have no idea why it went off, the house is still secure."

My cell phone rings by my bed, assuming it must be the alarm company. I sprinted towards our bedroom nightstand and got it just before it went to voicemail.

"Hello Mrs. Morgan, this is Lone Star Alarm Company wanting to check in with you in regards to your alarm going off. Is everything alright?"

"Ummm… Yes," I say, so damn flustered. Reaching for the alarm clock, I see it reads 3:41 am. Of course, it does. I am sure the alarm started at 3:39 am.

"No…No, please don't send anyone. We can't figure out why the alarm went off anyway," I say.

"Why don't we start with your family password to verify this account?" My mind is blank for a second. "Oh, yeah, it's Spinner." Mitch was a dedicated fisherman and picked the password himself.

"Thank you. Ma'am, this may sound strange, but my systems indicate the windows on the first floor were triggered and all opened at the exact same time. It must be a malfunction with the alarm system because you have nine windows on that floor. This makes no sense. If you don't mind, we would like to send a technician out around noon today to see what's going on."

"All windows at the same time?" I say with concern and a sick feeling to my stomach.

"Yes, ma'am, and because of this we won't send police out just because it looks like a technical issue."

"Thanks," I say, still feeling shaky and sitting on the bed.

"Today at 9 am someone will be out to fix this issue. My apologies again. Like I said, I've never seen this before."

"That sounds fine, have a good night." I sit back on the bed, taking in all this madness.

"What did they say?" Mitch asks, standing at our bedroom doorway with his baseball bat resting on his shoulder. I look over, shaking my head.

"You can put that away now, apparently it was a malfunction with the system because he said all the main floor windows were tripped at the same time."

"That's weird, isn't it?" He asks.

"Umm yeah, I would say so." I put my phone down and stand up.

"No need to get up, I tucked the kids in already. Thanks for saying I set the alarm off to them." He laughs.

As I sit back down, my phone starts to ring. The caller ID says it's Carol. "Oh great, it's Carol. The whole neighborhood must have heard."

"Hello, Carol!" I answered. "No, we are all fine, just a malfunction with our alarm system. No, really, we are okay. Sorry about the noise. Yes, we can chat tomorrow, goodnight." I hang up and lay back in bed. "Great I'm sure everyone will be buzzing with chatter tomorrow," I say to Mitch.

"Who cares, let's get some sleep," Mitch says, rolling onto his side of the bed. He always has this superpower to fall asleep anytime, anywhere. It must be nice.

CHAPTER 11

Daylight creeps in rather fast, and yet again, I never went back to sleep. Laying there, I listen to Mitch's snoring and let my mind wander. I get up and head to the kitchen to make a fresh pot of coffee. Mitch has a big conference call today, and I feel bad for his lack of sleep. Pouring myself a piping hot cup of coffee, I inhale the aroma. Mitch walks into the kitchen and kisses me on the cheek, pulling me into him for a hug.

"Don't spill my coffee, this is liquid gold!" I chuckle.

He lets go, "I'm going to need a couple pots of that liquid gold today, my call is at 8 am."

"What's it about?" I ask.

"Not sure," he replies. "I think new territory." He pours himself a cup of coffee and takes a sip. "Perfect," he says with approval.

"I better have a shower and get the boys up for school. Good luck babe," leaning in for another kiss.

"Thanks!" Mitch smacks my butt while I walk away, and I head to the bedroom with an eye roll and a smile. He may be cheesy, but I sure love him.

I drop the boys off at school and drive back onto our street. Today I was dreading talking to Carol and the alarm company; it surely is a crappy way to start today. Sure enough, as I pull into the driveway, Carol's sitting on my doorstep. Stepping out of the truck, I start walking towards her.

"Dropped the kids off already? You're faster than me!" I say.

"Yeah, I wanted to bring a peace offering." She hands me a Starbucks.

I smile. "You didn't need to do that." I accepted her coffee. I'm going to need every ounce of caffeine today.

"Yes, I do, Becca. Last night was silly and I apologize for it."

"It's okay, it was fun until it went south with the topic of my house."

"Yeah it was silly, and speaking of your house, what happened last night?"

"The alarm company said there was some malfunction with the windows, they are coming back this morning to fix it. Sorry, didn't mean to wake up the whole neighborhood."

"I'm just glad you're alright. Listen, I have to run. I have a trainer today at the gym." She gives me a hug and smiles.

"Thanks for the coffee, Carol."

"Anytime, doll!" and just like that, she disappears inside her house.

I open the door to our home and can hear Mitch on his conference call in his office. Quietly, I close the door and head right to our room to make our bed and start getting ready for the day. Not long after, Mitch walks in. I look up at him and see him rubbing his head.

"How was your call?" I ask.

"Umm, it was okay. We have taken on some new territory."

"Oh, yeah, that's great, where?"

He is hesitant to say. "Canada," he replies.

I look at him and can read him like a book. I've only been through this a million times. I sit down on the bed. "So what does that mean?" Not ready to hear his answer.

"Nothing really. It just means this is something I have to do, so I will be traveling a bit more."

"Bit more? Like how much?" He already travels so much it would be hard to think of him away even more.

"They are also giving me the opportunity to relocate back to our home town in Kelowna, BC."

"What?"

"They didn't say we had to, they just gave me the option. They say having someone in Canada would be our future goal and I could even open an office."

At this point, my mouth is sealed, and my eyes are directed at him. Yes, moving sucks, but I'm not going to lie; being back in Kelowna, where both our families live, sounded like heaven.

Kids growing up in the same city as their grandparents is the best memory, even from my own childhood.

"We can talk about it later, it's an option. We have been here for a bit now and it's a new adventure for our family. We know how much we like those, plus the kids are at the small age right now where we can get away with another move."

"Mitch, stop. You don't need to sell this to me, I get it. I'm 100% supportive of whatever we need to do. I would follow you to the end of the earth and back. No, wait, I take that back." I giggle playfully.

"Very funny," he says, pushing me over on the bed. Just then, a loud smash comes from upstairs, right above our heads. It's Connor's room.

"What the hell was that?" Mitch says as he gets up, darting out of our room and up the stairs. I'm following right behind him. He opens Connor's door, and we get a gust of wind. The window was completely shattered, and glass was everywhere.

"What the hell is this?" Mitch looks at the window. There wasn't a piece of glass in the window frame. It looked like it exploded, leaving a litter of small fragments of glass in every corner of the boy's room.

"What did this? Birds?"

"I don't see a thing," he says as he steps over the glass.

"Great, let's just keep adding the disasters to this house. I'm going to call a window company and get it replaced before the boys get home."

Mitch storms past me, and I'm left standing there staring. *What the hell happened?*

I start ripping the sheets off and remove items from the room. This will be an all-day cleanup.

My mind wanders to our conversation before the window. Kelowna would be nice; it would mean a possible end to this madness.

CHAPTER 12

After the alarm company spends two hours in my house trying to find what went wrong, they left with no answer. They couldn't find a single reason for the alarms going off. They said everything was fine, and maybe the wind on the window panel triggered the alarm. I wasn't even attempting to argue or tell them it wasn't windy last night. Deep down, I knew the reason.

Mitch managed to get someone out to replace the window rather fast; he too did not offer an explanation as to why the window shattered into our son's room. All my mind kept wondering was the possibility of moving back home to Kelowna. We were also lucky the rental company reimbursed us right away for the window, knowing I couldn't exactly wait for the ticket to be made and distributed. I needed a window replaced immediately, and I got just that.

There is one hour left until I have to pick up the kids from school and I want to call my mother. She would be over the moon with excitement over Mitch's offer, but I also wanted her to calm me down with everything going on in this house at this very moment. Plus, I'm completely alone, so an undisturbed phone call is just what's needed.

"Becca, that's amazing news! You know how much I would love my grandkids closer."

"I know, Mom." I let out a small smile while talking to her. I knew this would make her day.

"I think it's time to come home and settle down, and more so get the heck out of this house, Mom. I'm always scared and not sure what's going to happen next."

"I told you Becca, something is not right with that house."

"I know, Mom. I've actually got used to some of the things going on here. Like when I'm downstairs and the kids are in school I can hear walking upstairs or toys going off. I just let it go, it's the windows exploding or night-time occurrences I can't handle. I don't want to see this little boy anymore, and is this a safe place for my kids?"

Just then, there is a disturbance upstairs that is now making its way down the staircase. I turn my head and see a blue ball bounce from the last step. My stomach instantly gets butterflies.

"Mom, listen, I have to go grab the boys from school. I'll keep you posted, I promise".

"Okay bye love, give the boys a kiss for me."

"Bye, Mom!" I hang up the phone and grab my keys. *I can go sit in a car line for 45 minutes, but I'm not waiting in this house.* Grabbing my purse, I open the door and step out. The heat hits my back as I close the door behind me and lock it.

Something hit the door on the other side with force. I know that sound; it's the blue ball bouncing off the inside of the door.

Someone is mad. I head to the car fast with an awful feeling that the worst is right around the corner, or in this case, the door.

CHAPTER 13

Weeks go by and so much changes. We have decided to take the offer and relocate our family back to Kelowna, Canada. It was rather an easy decision but a decision that comes with so much work.

"Mitch, I'm serious, this house gives me the creeps. Something is going on here."

"You need to stop, I don't believe in this supernatural stuff. We will be out soon enough, and we can start packing. Our move back to Canada will be great for everyone."

"I get that Mitch, but until we move you are still traveling and being gone for 5 days at a time. It is a long time for me to be alone in this house with the kids and whatever else is going on here."

"Becca, you will be fine and if something comes up head to a hotel if it makes you feel better."

"Fine," I say, completely understanding I've lost this battle.

Mitch grabs the suitcase handle and pulls it to the front door. "Boys? I'm leaving, come give Daddy a kiss goodbye." The boys run downstairs and race to Dad, grabbing onto him with a good squeeze. "Now listen boys, you are the men of the house until I get back, you understand?"

"Yes, we understand Dad. That means we are the boss."
They both look at me and smile.

I shake my head, "Not likely my loves, Mom is the boss of
this house."

Mitch laughs and leans over to give me a nice long kiss.
"I'll be back as soon as I can, I love you."

Fixing the collar of his jacket, I smile. "I love you too, text
me when you land."

Mitch opens the door, and the Texas heat pushes its way
into our air-conditioned house. We wave at the door and close
it as Mitch turns the corner to head to the driveway.

"We're the boss of Mom… We're the boss of Mom." The
boys sing while dancing around me, celebrating.

"Good grief," I say and roll my eyes. "Who's ready for the
pool?"

"I am!" screams Connor.

"Let's go get changed, then Mommy is going to start
packing."

We head outside, and the strong sun feels so good on my
skin. The boys are jumping into the pool's deep end. Logan
launches on the surface of the water; his life vest makes him
bob in the water. They sure love this life of pool, sunshine, and
friends. The upcoming movie will be another adjustment. The
boys pull themselves to the edge and get out of the water,

sopping wet. They bend their knees getting ready to launch off of the side of the pool again, when we are interrupted by an alarming sound coming from inside the house.

It's Mats, our tiny chihuahua, yelping like he's being attacked from the inside of the house. Connor looks at me with a very concerned face. "Mom?" All three of us run to the back door as the yelping gets more violent with the sound of glass hitting the floors. *Did someone break into our house? Is someone hurting my dog?*

"Kids, get behind me!" I reach for the doorknob, and it's locked. Who locked our door?

"Come on boys, quick," I say as I usher them to follow me.

"Mom, I'm scared."

"It's okay, Connor, maybe Mats is just being silly." I always leave a window open on the main level. Mitch hates it because we have the air conditioning on, but sometimes a bit of fresh air in the morning is what the house needs. We run along the side of the house, and sure enough, the window is open. Mats has stopped yelping, but now I can't hear him at all. Sick to my stomach and shaking badly, I pry the screen off the window. Stepping in. "Mats?" The boys are at the window pushing their heads in to see, but they are not stepping in. Taking two steps, I can see glass all over my kitchen tile from dishes that were in my cabinets. Right beside the island in the kitchen was Mats lying on the floor. His eyes were open; he was breathing fast but not moving. No one is here.

"Mom, we are coming in." I look back and see them crawling inside. I head back over to the window to help the boys place them in a safe place away from the broken glass.

"Is Mats okay?" Connor asks.

"I think so!" I kneel down next to Mats. He lets out a small whimper and lifts his head. "What happened buddy?" Mats sits up and shakes his head, climbing all over me, whimpering; he looks terrified. Picking him up, I look over at the boys.

"See? He seems okay. Why don't we get changed and take him over to our vet and to him looked at?" The boys agree and immediately start removing the wet swim trunks right there on the spot. "Run upstairs and put your clothes back on, they are on the bed." The boys dart for the stairs while letting out giggles. Standing there, I am holding Mats, who is still shaking.

"What happened little buddy?" Glancing around, I check all the other windows and doors. Everything is locked, and I honestly have no clue what happened.

We are waiting for the vet to come into our room after looking over Mats. The door opens, and a tall man in his 30s steps in wearing a long white coat.

"Mrs. Morgan, I have looked over Mats and can honestly say I'm not too sure what happened to him. His vitals are good, and his heart rate has come down. He seemed rather stressed when I first saw him. To me, the injuries are superficial. I would usually say that maybe it was a result of being thrown around during play and maybe hitting something."

I frown. "This didn't sound like playing, more like an animal screaming in pain."

"If you don't mind, we would like to keep Mats for observation. He has calmed down dramatically and is now sleeping. I would feel better monitoring him to make sure seizures are not playing a role either."

"This makes no sense." grabbing my keys in frustration. The boys follow my cue and stand up to leave.

"I'm sorry, I don't have anything else for you, but know we will take very good care of him overnight." My eyes tear up, and I take the boy's hands as I'm heading out of the room.

"Thank you!" I say.

"Mats isn't coming Mommy?" asks Logan.

"No, baby. The doctor wants to make sure Mats is all better before he comes back home."

"Mom, I don't understand what happened to him."

"I don't know either, baby, but at least we know he is okay, right?"

"It was the zombie Mommy, he's mad."

I look over at Logan. "No, there is no zombie. Now enough of this talk, what about some ice cream?"

"Yeah!" Both boys yell in excitement. I just needed to distract the boys from the zombie topic because maybe Logan might be right; I think someone is mad.

We are back home after a big bowl of vanilla ice cream with sprinkles; it seems to cure almost anything. The boys are in my bed for the sleepover since Mitch is away and out like lights. I'm taping the bottom of boxes and getting them ready to fill with our belongings, to start the packing process. The best time to work is in the dead of the night when the house is quiet, and all I hear is the noise of the dateline on the TV. It is probably not the best show to watch with Mitch gone and all the unexplained things going on, but it's a distraction while I pack. The house remains silent while I fill the boxes with my books and living room decor. I tape the top tight securing and labeling 'Living Room Decor' on the box. Four full boxes are done, and I realize how truly exhausted I am. Walking toward the wall, I turn on the alarm system and turn off the lights.

Tomorrow I'll pack my photography room and the kids' playroom. It should be done in less than a week. I walk into my room, closing the door behind me, making sure to lock it. My phone beside my bed pings, and as I walk over to grab it, I see the boys are almost cuddling each other, sleeping. Logan lets out a tiny snore. Picking up my phone, I can see it's Mitch.

"How are things?"

"Everything is fine, I'm heading to bed now. Love you.".

Mitch texts back. "Night babe, see you in four days."

I told Mitch earlier about Mats, and he was concerned, but of course, he has a reason for everything. "Baby, he's 13 years old, he's probably having a seizure." I was so deflated and tired I didn't even respond. I put my phone down and lay down in bed; my eyelids are so very heavy. Closing them, I drift off into a deep sleep.

"Mom, wake up! I want pancakes." Opening my eyes, I can see the sunlight is coming through the blinds.

I never woke up in the middle of the night? Was the house silent? I feel like a million dollars. I roll over, and Logan is in the middle, still sleeping and Connor on his side facing me. "Please Mom, pancakes?"

"Sure!" I say, smiling. How can I say no to this perfect little face?

Logan stirs and rubs his eyes. "Mom can I have a birthday cake for breakfast?"

I laugh. "No to Logan's birthday cake, but pancakes will be ready in ten."

Sitting up, I check my phone. Mitch's first-morning text has come in. "Love you baby, have a great day and talk to you after my meetings." Putting down the phone, I stand up, heading to my hanging housecoat. I really do feel great. Tying the belt around my waist, I open the bedroom door. Walking around the corner to my living room, I look up, stopping completely dead in my tracks. The four boxes I had packed are completely unpacked, and my books are lying all over the floor shredded into a million pieces; it looks like snow all over my living room. The living room glass decor was back on the shelves where I took them from, but the books were completely destroyed.

"Look Logan, it's Christmas." The kids push past me and pick up handfuls of novel paper, throwing it high above their heads and letting it fall to the floor. Glancing around at all the doors, I can see they are locked, and the alarm system is still armed.

"Boys, Mom is going to take you to Carol's after we eat, Mom has some cleaning to do."

My legs are shaking, but this is not a time to lose it. I'm going to not react at all. Stepping over the mess and into the kitchen, I pull out the bowls for the pancakes. *What excuse can Mitch come up with for this one?* I wonder.

CHAPTER 14

"What? There is no way, Becca. That's impossible. You have had so much on your mind with the move, Mats, and not sleeping. You must have dreamt you packed." I listen to him on the phone. How bad is it that I don't even want to argue about this anymore? What's the point? It's a losing battle, and I have never won yet.

"Yeah, probably," I say, rolling my eyes, ending that conversation.

"Listen, Becca, I'm walking in to the meeting. I'll call you later."

"Love you." I hang up the phone.

The boys have been over at Carol's for a couple of hours while I clean up the insane mess of paper all over the first floor. The books that were entirely destroyed were ones I've had for a very long time, passed down from my family. Now they are all gone, my heart ached. Making my way to the front door to grab the kids from Carol's, I notice one tiny piece of paper ripped from a book. *I must have missed this one somehow.* I bend down and pick up the paper to see one tiny word on it. "Forever," I say out loud. *Forever.* My hand crumbles it up into a tiny ball, and I think to myself, *not freaking likely.*

The boys fly through the door at a swift speed and run straight upstairs laughing.

"Mom is heading to the camera room to pack."

"Sweet," says Connor, "Let's grab some army men and make a base in Mom's room." *Good, that should keep them busy while I pack.* I drag a couple of empty all-ready, assembled boxes and bring them upstairs into my camera room. I love how the room is set up all over with photos of my grandpa and me, full of so many memories. This is how photography started for me. My grandfather and I would take some shots and then discuss what we did to get that effect. He would always find the oldest camera he could and buy it off eBay, so proud of his new find. It was a joy we shared until his last days when he left us too soon. He left all his cameras to me after he passed, which meant the world to me, but never filled the void I had in my heart.

"Mom, how old is this camera?"

"Old, Connor, this one is Ansco's Buster Brown 2A. It's an antique folding camera made around 1912."

"Is that as old as you, Mom?"

"Cheeky little bugger, no."

He giggles. I'm holding the body of the camera covered in leather, letting out the smell of vintage beauty, making sure it's packed well with some bubble wrap. *I would be crushed if something ever happened to any of the cameras.*

"Logan! Put that down…Mom!"

"It's alright, Connor." I walk over to Logan and see he's picked up another one of my grandfather's cameras. With the Pentax SLR camera out of his hands, I take a look at it. Pentax is one of the greatest and longest-lived cameras. This one has been well-loved. Taking off the lens cover, I bring it up to my eye. It still has the sharp, clear focus, and then "click." The camera goes back to ready mode, and I look down to see that there's film in it.

"What?" I whisper. My grandfather must have gotten this old one working and started taking photos. A jump of excitement runs through my blood. What if I have some more pictures of him? It's like I can see what he saw when he took those photos. What beauty captivated him? *He never finished the roll, and there must be just a couple of snaps left.* It puts a soft smile on my face. It's a gift from the heavens. Packing is no longer important to me. I head to the door with the camera in my hand. "Boys, Mom feels like celebrating. Let's make some homemade pizza and have a fun movie night."

"Yeah!" the boys scream as they drop their army men and leave them on the floor. "Let's go!" they say and start running past me. I want to call Mitch; what a gift this is. A gift from the heavens, a gift from my Pa.

The night swoops in fast. After a pizza and movie, the boys are now crawling into my bed. Still in awe from the camera, I have now taken it into my bedroom and placed it next to my bed. I set on the alarm system and close the curtains.

"Mom... what do you think my great grandfather took pictures of?" Connor asks.

"I don't know, baby, but I bet you they are something special... like you" I pick up the camera and bring the boys into focus. "Cheese!" they both say with cute little smiles. I snap a photo and can hear the sweet sound of it getting ready for another picture. There must be just one or two more photos left, and then I can get the roll developed. I'm not even sure where I can go for that. I have not developed any film in such a long time. The digital world just took over.

"Okay, boys, it's bed time." I put the camera back down on the nightstand and snuck into bed with them. Everyone is tired, and the conversation is almost non-existent. We just listen to each other's breathing, drifting off into a deep sleep.

The sunlight shines through the tiny gap left by the curtains. I wait for my eyes to completely adjust and look over to see both boys still in a deep slumber. Looking at them reminds me of how happy these kids make me feel, no matter what house or city we live in. As long as these sweet babies have a smile on their faces, that's all that matters to me. I reach over to grab my phone and see what time it is. I bump my camera. The excitement runs through me again, remembering the film that I need to develop—the *gift from the heavens.* My phone's time reads 8:09 am.

"Wow!" I say out loud. I actually slept all night long and slept in. So did the kids; I guess it was much needed.

I pulled up a new window on my phone started my search for a business that can develop the film. Darkroom Processing is located in Grapevine, TX. A little bit of a drive, but it will be worth it.

"Mom… Can I have Lucky Charms for breakfast today?" asks Logan rubbing his sweet eyes.

"Are you feeling lucky, Logan?" I roll over and tickle his sides. He giggles and responds, "Yes!"

"Okay then, let's have some breakfast and then Mom has got some running around to do. Then we need to start packing up your rooms."

"It's not my room, Mommy, it's the zombies room."

That thought just gives me such a heavy feeling. "No, baby, that's your room and we will need to pack it all up for Canada."

Connor opens his eyes and looks over to Logan. "Don't worry, Logan, he can stay here."

"Enough talk about zombies, boys, let's enjoy some breakfast and maybe a cup of coffee."

"Ewwwww, I don't want coffee, Mom!"

"Me either," says Logan.

"Good, more for me then." I smile.

We all crawl out of bed and open the bedroom door heading out to the living room. My anxiety starts surfacing as I turn the corner to see the living room. Letting out a sigh of relief, it's all still packed up. Boxes on top of boxes just like how I left it. I pour the Lucky Charms in two bowls, thinking last night was rather quiet. Maybe we are finally turning a corner.

CHAPTER 15

The drive to Grapevine felt so long and difficult. Logan always has ants in his pants and makes any drive over 20 minutes feel like an hour. Traffic was heavy, and the sun was hot. My Dodge Ram was bought back home in Calgary, Alberta. It has the best heater for those freezing cold -30 C days with snow, but my air conditioner just barely does it here in Texas. We are only a month away from being picked up and railed back up to Canada. This truck sure has traveled everywhere.

We pull into the parking lot of The Darkroom, and the boys cheer. "We are finally here, Mom? What is this place?"

"Connor, this is a 'no-touch' zone. I'm sure there will be a lot of expensive stuff and if you break anything it would be very bad."

"This sounds boring," says Logan.

"I'll make you a deal." I turn around and make eye contact with both boys. "If you both are good in this store we can get ice cream on the way home."

Looking at each other, they both smile, and they make a silent agreement. "Okay, Mom. We will be the bestest."

I check my bag to make sure my camera is in it and hop out of the truck. Opening the back door for the boys, they jump out and run to the front glass door of the store. We walk through

133

the door with a chime from the bell and do a quick scan. There is nothing the boys can get into, only lots of glass cases that undoubtedly require some Windex after the boy's hands have been all over them.

"Hi there!" I'm greeted by a tall, middle-aged man with dark hair. He takes a look at the kids and lets out a laugh. "Looks like you keep your mom on her toes, boys."

"Do they ever?" I say and smile.

"What can I do for you today, ma'am?"

I reach into my bag and pull out the Pentax. "I inherited this from my grandfather and while packing last night I realized it still has film in it. I was wondering if I can get it developed?"

"Sure, not a problem."

I hand the camera over to him. "I didn't want to open it and take the film out myself just in case I did something to the roll and ruined it. I'm hoping for some last pictures of my grandfather, or to at least enjoy what he saw."

"Don't worry. I will make sure to carefully take the roll out. You know, these old cameras are sure something. Sometimes I think you still get better photos from film then digital."

"I agree," I say and look around to see the boys playing tag in some empty space. It is not the best game for a store, but hey, it keeps them quiet, and no one else is in to shop with us.

"I think there may be some photos left to take, I forgot to use the last little bit of the film this morning."

"Nope, all exposures were used, and I have nothing this morning, so I can get them developed here in a couple hours if you want."

"Really? That would be great."

"Sure thing. Come back in a bit and pick them up."

"Alright boys, how about that ice cream?"

"Yeahhhh!" They scream and head to the door.

"See you lads soon."

The kids are eating their Dairy Queen ice cream, and it's reminiscent of moments of when my grandparents would take my sister and me to the Dairy Queen as young girls. It was always exciting picking which colored booth to sit in and who would get the brain freeze first. My mind gets distracted with that memory when my phone vibrates in my purse. The call display shows it's my mom.

"Hi, mom...Yeah, no, the house has been very quiet. Nope, nothing new. I have the house about 80% packed. I just have to do the kids rooms, finish my camera room and one more box from the kitchen. Nope, Mitch is home tomorrow and he's booking our one-way tickets home. I have to grab Mats from the vet on the way home after this. Listen, I'll call you back in a couple hours. Love you too."

Putting the phone back in my purse, I realize we have enough time for the well-shaded park we passed on the way to Dairy Queen. It will give them enough time to burn the sugar off and maybe squeeze a nap on the long drive back home. The boys finish their ice cream cones with messy faces. "Boys, let's head to the park for a little bit before we head back to the store."

"Yessss! Thanks, Mommy."

We enter the front doors of the Dark Room with red faces. "You boys look like you had some fun!" The man behind the counter laughs. "Here are your photos, ma'am—singles of each 36 exposures.

"Thanks so much!" I grab the envelope and can feel the excitement run through my fingers as I place it in my purse.

"Let's ring you up here." He walks to the till by the front door.

"Mommy, I'm tired," Logan says. "Me too, Mom," says Connor.

I pick Logan up and get the receipt. "Thanks so much," I reach for Connor's hand.

"Have a great day, boys." The gentleman waves goodbye.

I put the kids in the car seat and buckle them up. Logan has already got his eyes closed, and Connor is now closing his. It looks like there will be a nap for the long drive home. We pull out of the parking lot, and I'm listening to my country radio station. Stuck at a red light, I glance over at the front seat and can see the envelope of photos at the very top of my bag. Contemplating if I should start taking a peek at some photos, I cave to my urge and grab the envelope. I've never been one to wait, and the excitement was taking over my body. Will I see my Pa?

The first photo is a tiny square of each 36 exposures, which I pass over right away. *Show me the good stuff.* The first, second, and third photos are scenery shots. I recognize it right away; it's Mission Creek Park, where my Nan and Pa would walk often. I even spent many hours on that playground as a little girl walking those trails. There are more scenery photos in the pack, and it brings such peace to my heart. These are images he thought were beautiful—moments he wanted to capture.

The light turns green, and I place the envelope of photos down on my middle console. *I am not done with you,* I think to myself. Looking in the rearview mirror, both boys are out cold. Sweet, another red light. I never thought I would be so happy to sit in traffic. There he is, a picture of my Pa. He must have accidentally snapped it in front of a mirror. He has his camera strap around his neck, looking down at it tinkering with the settings. His typical white hair and his blue jeans and sweater make me miss him so much. Then, there's the photo of my darling boys I took yesterday right before bed with their adorable smiles and arms wrapped around each other. The last couple of photos are blurry. It looks like maybe a finger got in the way? Another one looks too blurry to even make out. The next is a blanket, I think, or a photo of the inside of my purse?

When the next photo comes up, every ounce of color drains from my face. Suddenly I am unable to breathe. I can't get the button fast enough to roll down my window and get some fresh air. "No… No... No, what is this?"

My hand lets go of the photo, and it falls on my lap. The photo is of the children and me sleeping soundly last night. The hot Texas air is distracting me, taking the nausea and panic away. My shaky hand grabs for the next photo. It's another close-up of the boys and me from another angle. The angle is directed from someone standing in the middle of my bed looking down. How did I not see this happen last night? Or feel someone on my bed? I suddenly jump to the sound of a loud truck horn behind me. "Come on, lady!" a man yells.

I throw all the photos to the passenger seat with a quick movement and put my window back up. According to the passing cars, I drive through the green light that has been green for some time. *This can't be happening; this can't be real.* I need to concentrate on getting home, realizing I have now just missed my exit. "Fuck!" I start to panic, almost feeling like I'm not even in my own body. My mind is so distracted. I give a quick glance in my rear views, and the boys are still sleeping, thankfully not hearing me dropping curse words left, right, and center. Finally, I'm on the right route. I avoid thinking about it until the boys are in bed tonight; I'll deal with this then. Right now, I just need to get us home. Warm tears are streaming down my face. Coming to the realization, this was never the ending of or turning the corner; this house was just about to climax.

CHAPTER 16

We had arrived home just a little over an hour later after picking up Mats from the animal hospital. The vet said he couldn't find anything wrong with him, and he was fine to go home with close monitoring. I didn't even ask additional questions and felt like walking in a daze after the photographs. The photos were left in the truck; I couldn't even bring them into our home. While the kids were having some playtime after their bath, it was the perfect time to call my mom.

"Yes, Mom, we were sleeping."

"Becca, you need to get the heck out of that house, I'm telling you, the energy is bad and turning."

"I know, Mom. We have a couple weeks left and then we are out of here. I'm going to show the photos to Mitch and get him to come up with an explanation on this one."

"Mom, it's story time!" yells Connor from upstairs.

"Listen, Mom, I have to go. Don't worry about me. I'll figure this all out. Love you."

"Love you, Becca, be safe."

The call ended, and I just sit there, defeated. I'm alone on the first floor of the house, and yet there's a feeling something is down here with me, watching and studying me. Not even giving it any more attention, I get up to head to the staircase.

As I walk away, from my peripheral vision, I see someone small running to my right towards the stairs. Whatever it was, it was following me.

At the top of the stairs, I walk past Logan's Zombie Room. I'm not even looking in that direction, afraid of what I'll see, or more like who I'll see.

"Let's read your favorite book," I tell the boys, walking into Connor's room.

"Mom, we can't find it anywhere. It was right here beside the bed where we left it. Now it's gone!"

"It has to be here somewhere, Connor. Let's check under the bed and on the shelf one more time."

The boys run to the shelf pulling other books off dumping them on the floor.

"It's not here, Mom."

Bending down to my knees, I look beside the nightstand and on the floor. I find nothing.

Lifting the bed skirt, I look under the bed. Hunched under the bed in the shadows of the far corner was the contorted boy gripping the book we had been searching for. His body bent unnaturally, smiling, revealing his black rotten teeth. The ghastly odor of rot and decay floods the room. In a split motion, he crawls to me at an abnormally fast pace aiming right towards my face. I jump back, letting out a terror-ridden scream, "Noooo!"

"Mom! What is it? What's wrong?"

Grabbing my chest as the sharp pain of panic takes over my body, then left watching at the bed skirt now hanging down. Nothing is coming out. Both boys are staring at me, not sure if I'm playing a game or if something is actually wrong. "Nothing boys... I was just saying nope, the book isn't there either." I get close to the bed and lift up the bed skirt peaking underneath. Nothing. "Let's read another book tonight in my room." As if I am going to let them stay upstairs after what I just saw under their bed. You better believe I'm going to have them close to me tonight where they are safe.

Mitch is having a dinner meeting, and the boys are settling in; *I think maybe I should get the photos from the truck and take another look, yes.* I run to the truck to grab the photos from the front seat and rush back in the house into my room, alarming the system. Taking a deep breath, I flip through the photos. Only a couple of them are of us sleeping. I'm staring at them and then look beside the bed. *This is where the angle from the first photo is shot at.* My side of the bed is about 1 ft from the nightstand. I check the angle, and it's coming from a lower angle than where I would have taken it from. Standing up, I start lowering myself to the angle in the photo. Lower and lower. The sudden wave of panic takes over as I figure out it's coming from the angle of a small child.

I grab all the photos, stuff them in the drawer and slam it shut. "I'm not doing this anymore, this is complete crap." Mats looks up at me and does a little sniff from beside my bed. "I know, buddy, we can't get out of here soon enough."

My cell phone rings right beside me, startling me. It's Mitch.

"Hi, babe!" I say, relieved from hearing his voice.

"Guess what?" he says.

"What?"

"I'm 22 minutes away from home."

"What? Really! You are?"

"Yep. I thought I would surprise you guys and get home tonight instead of tomorrow afternoon."

A flood of emotion takes over my body. Relief, comfort, and the feeling of safety bring tears rolling down my face once again today.

"Becca...You there? Are you okay?" He laughs.

"Yes...Yes, I am!" I smile. "I just really missed you."

"Turn the alarm off. I'll see you soon." We hang up. Thank God Dad is almost home. "Everything is going to be okay," I say out loud while I disarm the system. "Everything is going to be okay."

***

"Becca, these photos are nuts, they actually creep me out! You didn't do this as a joke on me, right?"

"Me? Are you kidding me? I'm clearly sleeping!"

"Very funny. You have tripods upstairs."

Sitting there, I stare at him with my mouth open. It's unbelievable he thinks I was playing a joke on him. He is unpacking his suitcase, and I'm sitting there stunned, shocked. Even if Mitch is grasping at logical explanations, I really do think deep down he knows it wasn't me. Right?

"Babe, whatever those photos are, it is creepy but let's talk about our move. So… my meetings went well, and we have officially tied up all the loose ends before our official move date. I thought I would book the flights tonight with you. One way to our new home. Getting excited?"

I'm still staring at him in disbelief. "Yes. You have no idea."

"Good!" He sits on the bed and opens the laptop.

"So, I think we should fly out Thursday three weeks from now."

Three weeks. Three more weeks, and then that's it. We are done.

"Book it!" I say.

I pick up the photos from the bed that Mitch tossed down and stuff them in the nightstand. "I can't wait to get out of here, Mitch."

"Me too," he says. Then a loud smash from upstairs and the piercing screams of the boys make us jump right out of bed. Mitch is the first to fly out the door and through the living room, pulling himself up the stairs at projectile speed. I'm only two steps behind him, giving it everything I have to get to the kids as fast as possible. Mitch gets to the top of the stairs and around the corner towards their bedroom. Right when I reach the top stair, an incredible force punches me square in the chest. The energy is so powerful it launches me in the air and down the stairs to the first landing, smashing off the wall rolling to a complete stop. I try to scream, and I can't get any air in my lungs. The pain is so intense; I can't breathe. I can't breathe.

"Becca? Becca!"

"Mommy!"

Mitch is in Logan's arms and holding Connor's hand leading him down to the first landing where I lay motionless. I can't speak. I let out a gurgling sound from the back of my throat; it is all I can do. The excruciating pain of my back and right arm is leaving me unable to move, then realizing my arm is pinned under my body. *Is my shoulder broken?*

"Becca... what did you do?"

My boys stare at me with fear in their eyes, and Mitch looks scared to even touch me. Behind them, on the top of the stairs, I can make out movement. There he is—the small boy standing at the top of the stairs, staring right at me. I watch him slowly squat down to his knees as he observes me in pain. He's studying me, feeding off my agony, enjoying his view.

"Here, Becca, I'm going to move you."

Pain shoots from my shoulder. "Mmmmitch, my arm, noooo." Slowly, I move my legs and shift from my side to my back. Glancing again at the top of the stairs, the small boy is gone.

"Here... sit up against the wall. Babe, you scared the shit out of me! What happened?"

Leaning against the wall, I start to calm down, steadying my breathing. "I…. I honestly have no idea."

"Mommy you fell... like my dresser."

"Your dresser?" I question.

"Yeah, the kids' tall dresser fell right over. Must have been top heavy or something from packing. Glad it happened while they were sleeping. I brought them up to bed just 20 minutes ago and I didn't see anything that would have made it fall over. I haven't even started packing that dresser."

"Let's get you downstairs and get some ice for you. Boys, let's head back to bed and I'll tuck you in."

The pain in my shoulder is throbbing now with the beat of my heart, but my chest feels bruised; it hurts to take every breath. Mitch hands over the ice pack, and I place it on my shoulder. "This is a hell of welcome home." He chuckles. I roll my eyes. "Let's get you to bed and I'll get some Tylenol. You seem okay, you don't need an ambulance."

"No, I don't!"

"You need to see the doctor first thing tomorrow morning to check that arm."

I nod. Mitch passes me Tylenol and a glass of water. I swallow it and shake my head. "I could have been really hurt, Mitch!"

"Yes, you could have been. I'm going to go back up and check on the boys."

"Did you fix the dresser?"

"Yeah, I just lifted it when I realized you weren't behind me. Let's avoid crazy medical bills before we leave back to Canada."

"You booked it, right?"

"Yeah, the second I got the confirmation the bang happened upstairs. I've had way too much Red Bull for this kind of stuff."

I watch Mitch leave the room, and a minute later, I hear him upstairs with the kids.

Something deep down inside is telling me that Mitch may be now starting to believe me.

I think the boy wanted to inflict serious pain on me. I could feel his anger with that violent shove that made me plummet down the stairs; so powerful.

Closing my eyes, I feel the throbbing of my shoulder slowly start to subside—just a couple of more weeks, not even.

CHAPTER 17

The next morning, I walk back into the house. I feel conquered, sore, and completely finished. I'm now in a sling and have been told to take it easy. Nothing was broken, thank God, but there was some severe bruising.

"Look, Logan, Mom has one arm now!" Connor points, and Logan stares at me, shocked as I close the front door.

Mitch smiles and shakes his head. "You poor thing!" He chuckles. "Thankfully we are almost all packed now because you would have a problem. I've done all these boxes while you were at the doctors. We should be set now."

Looking over to the wall, he now has a dozen boxes packed stacked on top of each other. The house is starting to look empty again.

"I booked a hotel for next week. The house is almost ready to go, and the movers will come and load all of our boxes storing them in a container until we are ready to leave. We can spend the last couple weeks in a hotel and get this house cleaned and ready to go."

I was so happy, almost choking up, letting out a smile of relief. "Really? So how many more days here?"

"Just a couple I think. I'm going to run out and grab some things. Why don't you take the kids over to the waterpark with

Carol? She came over looking for you and I told her about your arm."

"Good idea!" I pick up the phone and call Carol. Playdate it is.

"Hello boys!" Carol waves from the grassy spot inside the waterpark. The boys run over to her and give her a big hug. "The kids are over there with the water guns, and I have two more super soakers ready and loaded for you." She hands them over, and they run off with big grins chasing their friends.

"Hi," I say, hugging her.

"Hi darling, how's that arm? I couldn't believe it when Mitch told me this morning. Thank Goodness you are okay. You know it could have been way worse? People die falling down stairs."

"Yeah. I could have broken my neck!"

"Come sit down over here with the ladies."

"Ladies?" I say. I had no idea anyone else was coming. She's leading me over to a cute setup of coolers, lawn chairs, blankets, and a picnic for all the children. She always thinks of everything. "How cute." Dropping my bag full of sunscreen, I look over and see a lot of familiar faces. All the ladies from my street. "Hello everyone!" I say with a wave.

"Hi, Becca, we heard about your arm. You poor thing. Come sit."

I grab a lawn chair, relieved to have a spot in the shade.

"We are sure going to miss you, Becca. Are you all packed now?"

"Yes, we are. The house is almost entirely packed now thanks to Mitch finishing it off since I'm kind if useless now. We plan on leaving the house the day after tomorrow and then stay in a hotel while we get the house cleaned."

"Don't you dare leave without saying goodbye." Carol points at me.

"Not a chance. We will be in and out all the time."

"It's sad. It was so nice to see that house with a family in it."

I frown. "That house?"

I watch Carol put her hand on the lady's arm as to say, "No, not now."

"It was a nice house and a shame we couldn't stay. It's nice to be heading back home to Canada near our family. We have never lived close to our family the last 15 years. The kids are at that age where they love to be close to the grandparents. My best memories were living so close to my family and heading to their house almost every day."

"Oh, for sure!" Carol agrees. "It makes sense and I bet your mom is over the moon."

"Yes." I beam. "For sure!"

I look over at the boys running through the water park; they will surely miss this too. Living here was great, other than the house.

"Carol says you had some crazy things happen in that house while you were there. We would love to hear about it. I totally believe in that stuff!" I look over at the lady, startled. I've only met her one other time, and she's all about what's going on in my life at the moment, especially the house. "Oh… nothing really. Only a few odd things here and there." I wave my hand to downplay the fact and hopefully guide the subject in another direction.

Carol pipes up. "Not really, Becca. You need to tell these ladies."

I look over at Carol, annoyed. *Why? Why do I need to sit and tell these ladies?*

"It was really nothing. Just a feeling and some odd things like lights and sounds."

"Sounds? What kinds of sounds?" They are intrigued now.

"Sometimes it was doors shutting, someone calling out for Mom, giggling, laughing and running upstairs. It was such a strange house and I'm glad to be moving on now."

They are just staring at me. Silently.

"What are you hens chatting about?" A man is walking up to us.

Carol stands up. "Mike, this is Becca."

"Nice to meet you, Becca!" He extends his hand for a shake.

"What are you doing here, Mike? Coming to cool down with the kids?"

"Me? No!" He Laughs. "Richie forgot his sunscreen so I just wanted to run it down. Teenagers nowadays. Can't remember a thing sometimes, I swear!"

"Becca is moving back to Canada in a couple days. She lived right next door to Carol. She was just telling us some crazy things that went on in her house."

I look over at the lady. That's such a stupid thing to say. Why would he care, and how dare you put me on the spot?

"It's nothing, really," I reiterate again, feeling everyone's eyes on me. I'm starting to feel set up.

"I always knew there would be sounds and things going on in that house," Mike pipes up.

I turn my head and look up at him, glaring. "Why is that, may I ask?"

"It was a pity of that little boy who died in that house so young some time back. It doesn't surprise me that the house is unsettled."

The air is getting sucked right out of me, and my stomach tightens.

"What boy? When? My house?"

Carol has panic in her eyes. She grabs my hand. "Don't worry about it, Becca. It's nothing and I was so happy to see the house with a family in it. I was so happy to see you and those beautiful boys."

I pull my hand from Carol's. "You knew? This whole time I was scared and terrified sharing my nightmares with you, and you knew about a death of a child, in my home!" I could feel the anger building up in me like a kettle.

"Everyone knew, Becca," says Mike. "The house was vacant forever after. The whole community knew. I write for the local paper and even have an article at home somewhere about the death of that boy."

I feel almost betrayed and lied to. "Everyone knew and didn't say anything to me? You don't think that's something I would want to know?" I stand up. Suddenly, I want to leave.

"Becca, we didn't want you to leave. We couldn't stand to see that house vacant another day."

One of the ladies stands up and reaches for some vegetables on the snack platter. The smell of ranch dip makes me sick, and tunnel vision is taking over my body. I hear the ladies yap back and forth about "the house", my home. "That house always gave me the creeps. I remember when I was walking the dogs and looked up to the second floor I swear I saw someone in the upstairs window."

"Here, Becca, sit down. Let's talk about the house. We can tell you everything."

"No!" I say firmly. "I've had about enough of listening to this shit and honestly… what kind of friends are you to keep this from me? I've got to get the kids home anyways."

I push past Carol. "Becca, please."

"She was bound to find out eventually, Carol. We kept it from her for a long time, I'm surprised it has only just come up."

"Becca!" calls Mike. "Listen, I'm sorry. I thought you knew. I feel terrible."

"It's fine. Mike. I'm out in two days anyways."

"Well, all the best to you and your family" He nods.

I force a smile and see the boys. "Boys… let's cool down at a movie theater. Does that sound good?"

The boys look at each other. "Yeah!!"

I would say anything at this point to get the kids out of this water park and away from the horror that I've just heard. I could use a cool dark place to think all of this through. A movie to distract the boys is just what I need. Good thing I packed a change of clothes in my bag. We hustle to the truck and open the door to a heatwave pouring out of the cab.

"Mom, it's so hot."

"I know, Connor. Let's get in and crank that air."

The boys climb in, and I walk around to my door. Carol is running towards me from the community exit calling out my name. Starting the truck, I pop it in reverse right away. I hit the gas, not waiting for her to make it to the truck to tell me a single thing, especially in front of my kids. The nerve of her! She gets smaller and smaller in my rearview mirror as I leave her standing alone in the parking lot. This was my life, my nightmare, and she knew the entire time, clearly using our conversations as topics in her book club meetings.

CHAPTER 18

"What? That's crazy, Becca. The realtor would have told us!" Mitch snaps. He's not taking the news very well. "Everyone knew? Why the hell didn't they tell us?"

"I don't know, Mitch, but shhh… please, don't wake the boys."

"I'm pissed!"

"I know. It says right here." I read off what my search on the computer brought up.

"In Texas, a seller or agent has no duty to release information related to a death by natural causes, suicide or accident unrelated to the condition of the property." I look up at him.

"So, what the hell does that mean? There could be a massive murder in this house, and no one needs to tell us? What happened to this boy? Becca, I would have never moved in here if I knew a child died in this house. A child!"

"I know. I know. I honestly don't know the details, Mitch. I left as soon as they told me. I didn't really want to hear another thing about it. This really freaked me out."

"Freaked you out? This is freaking *me* out. We have two more days in this house. How the hell am I supposed to sleep here knowing this now? Becca, I'm so sorry I didn't listen to you from the beginning about this. Why did they have to tell us now and not wait till we are out?"

"It's okay babe, we can get through this."

I'm looking up at him, agreeing with everything he's saying. This is really getting to him as he's pacing around the kitchen. Finally, everything has clicked for him, and now there is a build-up of concern in his eyes.

"Okay, I don't want to talk about this until we are out of this house. Promise me, Becca. No talk of this until we are completely out."

I nod. "Yes. I can do that."

"Alright. I'm going to go for a nice evening swim, and I would love for you to join me. We won't have a pool for much longer and a swim and a soak sound like something we can enjoy right about now."

"Sure. I'll meet you out there in a sec."

Mitch grabs his swimsuit and heads outside after he changes.

I look at the laptop screen in front of me. I type in the Google search engine:

Death at 1220 Greenway Close Texas—Nothing comes up.

Child dies in house at Greenway Close—Nothing comes up.

Why can't I pull anything up? Just then, there's a small knock at the door. Looking up from the laptop, I stare at the front door. Pushing my chair from the table, I debate on ignoring the door or going to open it. I'll just answer it. Walking towards the door, I put my hand on the doorknob, and I look through the peephole. I see no one.

I turn the door handle, opening the door slowly. No one is there, only the sound of the night bugs buzzing. Stepping out, I look around the yard, then the street, not seeing a single person. When I turn around to go back into the house, something bumps my feet. As I look down, there's a cut-up piece of paper under a rock. It's an article. The bold words on the top of the article read: CHILD DIES IN HOME IN OUR SMALL COMMUNITY.

I sit on the front step of our porch with the article in my hand. The cool evening breeze gently touches me, giving off a refreshing boost of cool air in my lungs. It's all real now. The article in my hand reads:

Jane Savannah, a mother of a young 7-year-old, found her son unresponsive a little after midnight last night. An ambulance was called to the 1200 block of Greenway Close, where a boy was taken to the hospital in cardiac arrest. He was pronounced dead later at SVH, where he died at 3:39 am. It's

not known why the boy went into cardiac arrest and was
unresponsive. An investigation is currently underway. Autopsy
to be done later this week to determine the cause of death. At
this time mother is not a suspect.

That's it? This gives me nothing. I fold up the news article
and take a deep breath releasing it as a sigh of loss and sadness.
The pain that mother would have endured and the sorrow this
house has felt… my eyes sting, glazing over with tears. *What
should I do? Two days left here; maybe I should just stop and
push through.* Just then, a branch snaps to my left. Startled, I
looked over, trying to adjust to the darkness. There is a tall
figure emerging from the yard.

"Becca? It's me, Carol."

Oh great, please, not now. She's walking right towards me,
and I hate confrontation. If I get up, she'll just stop me
anyways.

"Becca, I feel like complete crap. I'm so sorry and
completely understand if you don't want to talk to me," There's
silence. I'm not answering because I'm not sure if I even want
to listen either. "Just hear me out, give me five minutes."

"Carol, you have five minutes and I have to go in." Carol
sits down slowly next to me. Something is weighing heavy on

her heart. She was such a great friend, and I will miss her, but she really did hurt me. I trusted her.

"Becca, I moved into my house a year after Stephanie, the original home owner, did. She had a wonderful little boy and a great husband. Years past and eventually the husband left her. I didn't know why, but she was completely distraught. She withdrew from all of us and hid in this house. I would wave when I saw her and Ryan, her son, but she would smile and go straight in the house. I got it. She wanted her own space."

I look over at Carol and can see her eyes full of emotion. "One night, I was awakened by flashing red lights in my window. I looked out and saw the ambulance outside her house. I ran out as they were rushing Ryan out on a stretcher giving him oxygen. Stephanie was following right beside him and I asked what happened. She never said a thing and looked right through me. The next day, I didn't see anyone and tried knocking on the door many times, hoping to see both of them. We never saw them at all. Later, I found out Ryan passed away the night he was taken by ambulance and not one person knew why. I never saw Stephanie either after that. From what I understand, she was so taken over by so much grief that she stayed in the house and never left. She never returned my calls or answered the door. I'm sure she never ate, never did the lawn, never went to get groceries. It was like she vanished. We all speculated because all we heard was that Ryan died and we never knew what actually happened that night. He was such a sweet boy, but after his dad left he became angry, probably lashing out missing his father. Regardless, it was heartbreaking."

"So… what happened? What did he die from? Most importantly why the hell didn't you say something as my friend, Carol?" The tone in my voice is announcing the irritation.

She sighs. "She stayed in this house until she was reported in the neighborhood for not taking care of her property. It was so dark, overgrown. Rats took over the house, the grass was dead and so high. Garbage bins left tipped over and litter on the driveway. No one knew what to do. We later heard from word of mouth that Ryan died from Long QT Syndrome, but that was never confirmed. I think it's a rare condition in which he apparently would never have any symptoms until it was too late. The house grew such a sad emptiness and carried such unresolved anger too. Eventually, I'm assuming, her family stepped in and came to get her. When they put the house up for sale and packed up her belongings, she was manic. I saw her leaving with her parents I think; she looked unrecognizable. Frail, pale, lost about 50 pounds and looked ill. She kept screaming because she didn't want to leave her house.

According to her, Ryan was still in the house and he would need her. It was heartbreaking watching this."

"That's horrible." I couldn't even imagine all her pain she felt.

"When the house sold, we were told by the new buyers that the whole house needed to be gutted. Carpet, walls, the entire inside had rotted away and full of rodent activity and mold. One day, I was watering the flowers in my front yard and out of nowhere walked up Stephanie next door. She had no emotion on her face and walked almost zombie-like to her front steps, she must have been medicated. She couldn't get back in the house because the locks had been changed by the new home owners while the renovations were happening. I'm assuming she just wanted the house that was once hers."

I'm staring at Carol in anticipation.

"I walked up to her almost uneasy, not sure if she was okay. I kept calling out for her, but she completely ignored me. Stephanie smashed her hand through the window by the door and unlocked the front door herself. There was blood everywhere; I had to call 911 for help. I never went inside the house to get her, I was too scared. I just let the professionals take care of it, and clearly she need professional help. They arrived a short time after and I guess she was talking to someone in the house, but no one was there. She stepped out of the house covered in her own blood and was so angry and aggressive at everyone in the yard. She kept saying she wanted to be left alone with her son, yelling at the cops to leave. No one could get close to her because she had picked up a shard of glass from the window and would wave it at everyone who came close enough."

"Carol this is crazy!" I'm shocked at what she's telling me.

"They eventually used the taser and apprehended her, she was a danger to others and even herself. They took her by ambulance. Last I heard, she was in a mental institution getting the help she needed. When she was inside the home she wrote "Forever" on the walls with her own blood, no one knew what that meant. Later, it was cleaned up again and repainted. The new buyers were so creeped out they never wanted to move in. The house was then given to a renting agency to take care of and maintain. The house kept that eerie dark feeling well after, that's when everyone started seeing odd things going on with the house. The lights would flicker like a strobe at night as we drove by late. Sometimes, I swear, I would see someone dart in front of a window upstairs and run away. I wasn't the only one. Almost everyone I knew saw or felt something walking past this house. After the renovations were done, we saw the house listed for rent. It was vacant for a long time until I saw your truck pull up. I thought this was just what the house needed, a beautiful family."

I feel lightheaded taking in all of this. That was us. The beautiful family walking into a madhouse that every single person on this street knew of.

"Don't hate me, Becca. I love you and the boys and didn't say a word because… I guess my own selfish reason. I didn't want you to leave. I wanted this house to have a positive energy again. This was everyone's favorite house to stop at on Halloween, kids doing dares and telling stories about it. It just broke my heart. This wasn't an attraction or fun house, this was a tragic story that needed to be left behind in the past."

My mind starts racing as I make sense of everything she is telling me. All the new house smell when I came in. The new carpet and paint. Just then, the door swings open, and Mitch is standing there. "What the hell is going on? Carol you better not be starting this shit up again. Why didn't you tell us?"

I stand up, swallowing all this information. "Mitch, stop. Let's go inside." I walk in front of him, and he takes a couple of steps back.

"Goodnight, Carol. I'll talk to you later."

She stands there, not saying anything holding her own hands with sadness in her eyes. I get it. I understand why she did it, but somehow I still feel betrayed. Would I have moved into this house knowing what I've found out tonight? Probably not.

"What the hell was she doing here, Becca?"

"Mitch, it's fine. She was just telling me her side. She's just —"

"Stop, I don't want to hear about this anymore. We have a full day here tomorrow and the moving company comes to load the day after. I can't get out of this house fast enough. I'm going to bed, are you coming?"

"I'll be there in a minute. I'm just going to check on the boys and turn all the lights out."

Mitch is already around the corner and gone. I'm left standing there soaking in all this information. I'm looking around at the front windows by the door where she put her hand through. What was she doing in this house? I start heading up the stairs to check on the boys. It's quiet and dark, just the moonlight coming through the windows. It's bright enough I don't even need to turn on any lights. I quietly walk towards Connors' room and open the door just a peak. The boys are fast asleep. Connor has his arms wrapped over Logan. Closing the door, I head down the hall and stop to see Logan's room with the door slightly ajar. Walking towards the room, I slowly open the door. The room is dark, and I sit on Logan's bed that he has never really ever slept in. I pick up a little bear from the bed and look at it. The blue furry little bear has the cutest black nose and brown eyes. I remember when we gave this to him when he was only a couple of days old. Warmth fills my heart, and yet I still feel heartbroken for everything that occurred in this house before us. The boxed-up bedroom feels so empty now and almost sad.

"Listen. I don't know if you can hear me. I don't know if this was once your room, but I want you to know I'm so sorry for what happened to you. I'm so sorry your mom got sick and had to move. You need to move on now too Ryan. Everything will be alright."

I sit and listen for a couple of minutes in silence. "Goodnight," I say.

Standing up, I place the little bear on the mattress. In less than 48 hours, this will all be a memory, one I would like to forget. Stopping at the top of the stairs, I listen one more time. Silence again. I head downstairs, making sure to grip the railing with my one good hand to prevent any other unexpected mishaps. I turn off the rest of the lights in the kitchen and check the doors and the window I usually secretly have open for fresh air. The alarm won't arm unless it's closed and locked. With the house now secure and the lights out, I head down the hall to the master where our bedroom room lights on. Maybe Mitch is still awake. Walking into the bedroom, I stop immediately at the doorway. There he is, the small transparent boy standing right over Mitch in bed. Mitch is fast asleep and completely unaware that a dead child haunting this family is now looming directly over him. I grip the doorframe with my nails to stabilize myself from the now spinning room. Watching in complete horror as the little boy I now know named "Ryan" turns his head and looks right at me with an ear-to-ear evil smirk, slowly turning his gaze back at Mitch. He lifts his right foot up, aiming it directly over Mitch's throat. As he gets ready to make the fast, abrupt motion to bring his foot crashing down on Mitch's windpipe, I let out a blood-curdling scream leaving my whole trembling clutching the walls. Mitch lunges straight up with his hands swinging, knocking over the glass of water on his nightstand. The boy is gone.

"Fuck, Becca. What is it? Fuck, look what I did, there's water everywhere!"

I grab my chest in relief, walking straight into the master bath, and grab a towel.

"So, what was your problem? You gave me a heart attack."

"Nothing... Nothing, I'm sorry."

Mitch has had enough. We all have. There was no way I can bring it up again when he's asked me not to. We are almost there. Almost out.

"Damn, Texas' bugs, Mitch. I'm sorry. It flew right in my face."

"Well, if you didn't leave the window open they wouldn't get in."

I make eye contact. He knows I leave the window open.

"I know you like to do that, Becca. We aren't in BC where it's normal to have windows wide open in the summer."

"I know, I know. I'm sorry. I just like fresh air once in a while in this house, I turn the air conditioner off for a bit."

"You can open all the windows you want once we get back to Canada. In the meantime, keep them closed."

"Promise!" I force a smile.

"Let's go to bed." He pulls back the blankets and motions me in, pulling me close to him.

I lay there, and the image that occurred five minutes ago plagues my head, those piercing black eyes full of anger and so much hate. Wiggling free from Mitch's arms, I sit up. "I'm sorry. I can't sleep. Mind if I read a little?"

"No. Go ahead." He rolls over, and I turn on the lamp. *Mind if I read all night?* I think to myself. *I'm not going to sleep tonight. I'll be watching over my family all night long. I can't ignore this feeling, this feeling that something just isn't finished.*

CHAPTER 19

A sound coming from upstairs abruptly wakes me up from a deep sleep. I glance down to the open book in my hand; I must have dozed off mid-reading. Pushing the covers back, I listen, not realizing I'm holding my breath as if breathing would muffle the noise from upstairs. The alarm clock reads 3:39 am. Oh, no, it's that time. I remember reading it in the newspaper clipping. It was the official time of death for Ryan. Panic takes over, and I stand up to head out of the room. Tiny feet run from one end of upstairs to the other into the playroom. Muffled giggling is now in the air, and I know the sounds of my children. Slightly relieved, it's my kids and not the ghost child. I head out of the room and turn back to see Mitch still fast asleep. He can sleep through anything from storms to earthquakes.

I enter the living room, and everything is still packed in boxes. Passing the kitchen, I reach the stairs. No lights are on, and that's a little odd for my boys to be playing in the dark, but hey, they must be content with the darkness. Going up to the top of the stairs, I look down the hall to see Connor's bedroom door wide open. In the opposite direction is the open concept playroom where every single thing is packed. We let the boys have a handful of toys that would travel with us, and the rest would be trucked back to Canada. Turning left towards the playroom getting closer, and I can see Connor standing in the darkroom with his back to me.

I whisper, "Connor." He doesn't move an inch and keeps his back to me. He looks so cute in those blue pajama shorts, but he is still just standing there facing towards the wall. "Connor, what are you guys doing? It's almost four in the morning." I take a couple of steps into the center of the room. I'm only a couple of feet from him now. "Connor, I'm talking to you."

"I'm playing, Mom," says Connor, but the voice comes from my immediate right.

I turn my head, and Connor is on the floor in between boxes with a car in his hand. I immediately realize that's not my son in front of me. I turn my head back, and the pale porcelain skin of the boy is turning in my direction with his usual dark purple circles under his eyes. I watch him lift his hand towards mine. Stepping away from him, I stumble backward, landing hard on the ground. Ryan, the boy, evaporates right in front of my eyes.

"Mom, don't be scared. He's my friend. He said you said sorry."

"What?" I'm trying to pull myself together. Is he talking about earlier in Logan's room?

Oh God, I think he is!

"He said that you were right, Logan's room was his. I told him he could have it back because we were moving." I can taste the vile burning up my throat. Please stop, don't say anything else. "He said no, we weren't moving."

"Stop! No more, Connor." I'm scared. No, I'm terrified. I fumble to get myself up off the ground and reach for Connor.

"It's time for bed. Everyone's going to be awake in a couple hours and you should have never gotten out of bed."

"He asked me to play, Mom, I never saw him before and he's nice. I don't think he likes Logan because Logan calls him a zombie."

"Stop, Connor! No more. I don't want to talk about this any longer." I take him to his room, where sweet little Logan is still fast asleep. I gently lift Connor over Logan, and I crawl into bed with him.

"Mom what are you doing? I'll go to bed, I promise."

"I know baby," I say as I pull the blankets over me and snuggle up to him. "Mom just wants to make sure you fall asleep."

Connor doesn't argue and closes his eyes, ready for sleep. Looking around the darkroom, I pray not to see him. I want out of here. One more night here would be impossible for me. I watch over both boys as they sleep, and this time I stay awake the last couple of hours until the sun peaks over the houses.

This nightmare is almost over, or so I thought.

CHAPTER 20

I crawl out of the kids' bed and tiptoe downstairs to the silent, undisturbed house. Walking into the master bedroom, Mitch is still asleep with the lamp on my nightstand on. He never even realized I got out of bed. Turning off the lamp, I head out of the bedroom quietly, closing the door behind me.

"Mom, how am I going to take my balloon with me?" I look at the bottom of the stairs and see Connor pointing to the high decorative window up above the front door.

"Oh, Connor, we can get a new balloon somewhere later." I look up at that red foil balloon which is still floating but stuck at that window. That balloon gave me nightmares for days after waking up with it by my bedside. How it still has air is beyond anything I can understand.

"You don't need that balloon!" I hear Mitch say. Mitch picked Connor up and lifted him over his head.

"Daddy, please!"

"Listen to your mom, Connor. How are we? Everything packed?"

I smile, handing him a cup of coffee. "Everything but the coffee maker. Once this is done, I can pack it all up. When are we leaving?"

"I booked a room for tomorrow, we can check in at 4."

Another night in this house. You have got to be kidding me.

"Listen, I have a couple things to do with the truck before it gets picked up. I'm going to get started this morning and then maybe we can grab dinner tonight?"

"Sure," I say.

"I'll take this to go then." Mitch leans in and kisses me. Before I know it, he is heading out the front door.

"Boys, now's the time to make sure everything is in a box and all taped up. Who wants to help me clean some bathrooms?"

"Ewwwww, no, Mom." Connor shoots up the stairs as fast as his little legs can carry him.

The afternoon creeps up so fast. With all the cupboards, bathrooms, walls, and windows cleaned; all that's left is the carpet. Mitch always gives me a hard time with cleaning. "No one can clean like Mom," he would always say to the boys. I look at it more like a curse. I would love just to relax but growing up in a very clean and organized home where my chores were always done and spot-on, led to my very first job as a housekeeper, but that just fueled my OCD with cleaning.

The boys have been playing so well all day and it's time for one of our last couple of dips in the pool. "Boys, pool time!" I hear a bit of an argument upstairs. *What on earth could they possibly be fighting about?* "Boys?"

Logan is the first to come down the stairs and in a hurry too. "Mom, Connor is talking to the zombie!"

"What?" I pick up Logan and yell upstairs to Connor.

"Connor!"

I can hear him saying, "Shhhhh."

"Yes, mom?"

"Can you come downstairs, please?"

Connor comes around the corner of the stairs and stands at the mid landing. "What!"

"What? Don't 'What' me. You don't talk to me like that. It's pool time."

Connor walks down the remainder of the stairs sulking, and heads to the bathroom where his swim trunks are hung up.

"Logan says you were talking to the zombie?"

"Logan is just a scaredy cat. I was talking to my friend and he's mad at me. He doesn't want me to leave. He also doesn't want me to go swimming."

I'm over this conversation of the zombie as so Logan calls him. "Well, too bad. This is my home and my rules."

"Yeah, well, your rules suck Mom!"

"Connor! Get outside now, what on earth has come over you?" I walk both the boys outside to the pool and watch as Connor dives in. Poor Logan is so quiet, I think he's unsure about the whole situation, witnessing his brother's poor behavior.

"He's mad, Mom," Connor yells from the pool.

Turning to him, I say, "That's enough." Logan's hand is violently pulled from mine, and he is yanked backwards from the back of his life vest. He flies three feet back in the air and lands, hitting his head on the brick corner of the house. "Logan! Oh, my goodness, Logan!"

He lets out a cry no mother ever wants to hear, and I couldn't scoop him up fast enough. With one hand still in the sling, I feel almost useless. The motherly instinct kicks in, and the next thing I know, is that I'm running him inside with Connor right behind me. Logan's head is bleeding dark crimson blood. With a cloth, I put pressure on it right away.

"Told you he was mad, Mom!"

"Connor, that's enough! No one is mad, we just need to get Logan to the doctor right away!"

Logan is screaming as I carry him out. The concern in Connor's eyes is evident as he grabs Logan's Star Wars bear heading out the door.

"Where are the keys to the truck?" I scream. My heart is racing, and panic is setting in. "I see Dad's car keys.... Wait... He has my truck. Let's take Dad's car."

We run out the front door slamming it behind us, and I unlock the car as fast as possible.

"Get in, Connor." He runs to the other side and slides in. Now, Logan's crying is more of a whimper, but I watch his eyes look at me with fear. It's only a seven-minute drive to the closest ER, but it will feel like the longest drive of my life.

We get home a couple of hours later with relief. The doctor said it could have been much worse, but Logan should be fine. No concussion, only a nasty bump on his head and some stitches. Logan must take it easy for today, enjoying some good Disney in Mom's bed. After putting on Monsters Inc., I wanted to phone Mitch back to let him know we are home safe.

"Becca? Are you home?"

"Yes, Mitch. Kids are in my bed but now I want to talk to you about something else. When are you home?"

"Not for another hour, I'm stuck in traffic. The truck is being picked up tomorrow morning along with our furniture."

"That's good. Listen. I don't want to be here in this house any longer. We are already packed and after today, Mitch, I'm not giving it another second in this house."

"Aren't you being a little much? We have everything booked for tomorrow. Listen, I hate this house just as much as you do but we can get through another 24 hours, don't you think?"

"No. The bags will be at the front door, Mitch. We are leaving tonight, see you in an hour."

As I am ending the call, I know I won this battle. The safety of my family comes first. We aren't talking about ghosts by my bed, under beds, or playing in the backyard. I'm talking about watching my son get yanked from my own hand. Maybe this spirit is mad. Maybe he doesn't want us to leave, but I couldn't care less. It's been a year too long in this house, and it's time to close this chapter of our lives. Everything is packed. The one open box in our room was for the bedding on our bed. Since we will not be staying the night, I throw it all in. Sitting on the edge of my bed, I hear someone running upstairs. Looking over at the boys in my bed, Connor and I make eye contact. Logan hasn't even noticed with his sweet head all bandaged up.

"Mom?" Connor says, looking at me.

"It's fine, Connor. We are just waiting for your dad." That hour went by so slow. It felt like two hours of sitting here listening to the running around upstairs like someone wanted us to notice them. The thumping, jumping, and tipping over of what sounded like packed boxes. Someone was throwing a fit; someone was furious. Ryan, the ghost child, was raging mad.

I hear the front door slam shut and I head out of the master to see Mitch walking into the kitchen.

"Who's over?" he asks.

"What do you mean?" I say.

"Who is over with the boys?"

"No one is, Mitch, they are in my room finishing up the movie."

"No. I just saw a kid upstairs looking over the banister when I came in. Blonde hair, blue jeans. He is this tall." He puts his hand out, showing the height a little above his waist.

"Mitch," I say, looking at him.

He stares at me, and it all starts clicking for him. He has finally seen the child. He has finally seen the boy who has been haunting me for a year. This is the moment he realizes this is all true, and this is the proof he needs. He saw Ryan.

"Grab the kids, get in the car!"

I turned around to head to the master, and thankfully the boys were already standing there. "Mom is it time to go now?"

"Yes, Connor, let's grab your shoes and head out."

Logan points up. "Balloon!"

"No, Logan, no balloon. We are heading to a hotel for some fun."

"Yay!" he says and thankfully drops the request for the balloon.

Mitch is dragging the two bags, and Connor is carrying poor little Mats out. Suddenly, we are all running for the car.

"We get to have a sleepover at a hotel, Connor," Logan says, all proud as Connor buckles his seatbelt.

"I know, I can't wait!"

Looking back, I see Mitch locking the front door, and a sigh of relief escapes my body. He's out. We are all safe and out of this horrible house.

"We have to come back tomorrow to let the movers in and to get the carpets clean. That's it, Becca. No more after that."

"Mitch, you saw him!"

"Stop, Becca. I can't talk about this right now. It freaked the F… out of me. I'm sorry I ever gave you a hard time. We can put this house behind us tomorrow and never ever talk about it again."

We both get in and Mitch starts the car. We pull out of the driveway and see the upstairs lights starting to flicker on and off. Looking directly at each other, we say nothing. We don't need to.

CHAPTER 21

This is the last day. We pull in the driveway at 7 am and sit there staring at the front of the house. I don't want to go in but know we have to. It feels like it was just yesterday walking around this house to see if it was a good fit for our family. To see if it could offer a safe and happy place to raise my boys. I should have gone with my gut and walked away from this house the second I stepped into it.

The large moving truck pulls in and the guys start laying down the blankets at the entrance of the house. Mitch walks in first, and he doesn't come out in a panic, so I know everything looks alright.

"Becca?" I hear to my left. It's Carol. "I made you up a little basket for the kids to keep busy, and a bottle of wine for you tonight. I'm going to miss you so very much. I'm so sorry about everything." She hands the basket to me, and I can see she has put a lot of thought into the gifts for the kids. It is full of crayons and books.

"It's okay. I will miss you too. This is something I will remember for a long time." I chuckle.

She lets out a smile. "Listen, while the movers load the truck, let the boys come over for one last play with the kids."

"Mom, can we, please?" both say, looking up at me, waiting on my next word.

"Yes, sure. Go right ahead!"

"Yayyyy!" they scream and run towards Carol's house. She turns, smiles, and chases after them.

This isn't a good place for kids right now anyways, with the movers lifting and carrying things out of the house. Hell, this wasn't even a good place for the kids a year ago. I should have gotten out sooner. Oh well, I'm done now, and that's all that matters. Walking into the house, I can see it's starting to empty fast. Some rooms are bare already, just in time for the carpet cleaners to get started upstairs.

"Ma'am, I'm sorry to bug you. One of your kids is in the room on the right, and he's crying, we can't get into the room to clean the carpets."

I stand there just staring at her. "Thanks, I'll go up." Obviously it wasn't my child. I made my way up the staircase, each step bringing me closer to a small whimper coming from above. At the top of the stairs, I look to the right, towards Logan's room. The door opens for me right away, slowly creaking open to see nothing. It's empty, vacant. Standing there for a minute, I don't hear anything else, no cry or whimper. I know what I need to do.

"Listen. I'm so sorry that you're stuck here and all you have gone through. We are leaving and I want you to do the same. You can't stay here haunting everyone. You need to move on. I'm so sorry, Ryan. I know you are mad and sad and probably lost. My family needs to leave this horrible house and you should too, it's time."

I wait; there's nothing after.

"Excuse me? Can I get in here and clean this carpet?" Glancing at the door, I see a large lady with a handful of cleaning equipment.

"Yes, sorry, go right ahead." Walking out of the room, I'm left with this unsettled energy, not feeling closure at all.

"Becca, it's all done. Everything is loaded and the truck was just picked up. Once they are done upstairs, we are good to go."

"Great. I'll go get the kids." I walk over to Carol's and knock on the door. She answers just soon after.

"Boys, your mom is here, time to go." A bit of sadness is in the air, and I hate goodbyes. "Boys, you be good for your mom now and I will talk to you soon, I'm sure!"

"Of course." They smile and lean in for a hug.

"Take care, Becca, and please keep in touch!"

"I will. Come on boys, off we go!" They head to the car, and I watch the cleaning crew lug their equipment out. This is it; this is goodbye. I wave one last time to Carol and walk to the boys who are already putting on the seatbelts, eager to start a new adventure. Tonight, it's an unusual cool Texas night with some storm clouds rolling in from the west. Walking around the car, I can see the front door wide open. I can see through the doorway to the back of the house where Mitch is standing there, frozen in one spot, just looking in my direction. Taking a couple of more steps towards the door, it's clear Mitch's face is pale and sweaty, as he's struggling to say something. He gets out the word, "B-B-Becca..." and the front door slams shut with extreme force. It shakes the windows on every level.

"Mitch!" Running up to the door, I fumble for the handle, and it won't budge. It's locked. "Mitch!" I bang on the front door, screaming.

Carol is coming over to see what the commotion is. "Becca, is everything alright?"

"Carol! Watch the kids!" I run along the side of the house and start looking in all the windows. The second I get to each window, the blinds close shut.

"Mitch!" I scream, banging on the glass with my fist. As I'm running to the next window, and for just a split second, I see Mitch still standing in the same spot with the look of terror on his face; what is he looking at? Then the blinds close.

"What the hell is going on?", I say, as I'm opening the back gate and running into the backyard around the outdoor counter. I turn the knob of the back door, but it's locked. I am banging so hard on the door, my hand starts to sting. Not sure what else to do, I sprint back to the front of the house to check on the kids.

"Becca, what's going on?"

"I don't know," I say, flustered and breathing heavily.

"Should I call for help?"

"No, not yet!" My heart is beating out of my chest when I hear Mitch yelling my name, banging on the other side of the door. The hair on the back of my neck sticks up, realizing he can't get out of the house. The house won't let him. Finally, for whatever reason, the door opens, and I am face to face with Mitch. He has lost all the color in his face as blood is gushing from his nose and down his chin.

"Oh, my God, are you okay? What happened?"

Glancing over Mitch's body, there are no physical injuries, just his nose; he's okay.

"He… He…. I couldn't move. He wouldn't let me!" Mitch was stuttering and shaking so much, that he handed me the keys. "Get in the car now! You drive, get us the hell out of here!"

Without questioning him another second, we run to the car. I give Carol a quick hug and get behind the wheel, leaving her questioning everything going on.

"Mom, Mom...what happened?" concerned Connor asks with wide eyes while staring at his dad.

"Nothing, baby, we are outta here!"

Mitch wipes the blood from his nose. "Go, Becca! Drive!"

Giving one last look towards Carol, popping the car in reverse and back out fast enough to lurch us to an abrupt stop. I accelerate forward past the house, with the tires letting out a squeal. Looking at the house as we speed off, there is no one watching us from the window. The lights aren't going on and off either. Letting out all of the air I was unknowingly holding in my lungs, I take a breath of relief. *It's over; it's all over.*

"Mitch, are you o—"

"Stop! I don't want to ever talk about this. Drop it!" Looking at him, I know he has realized how tormented I was by the child's lost soul. The boys giggle in the back seat, and it breaks my attention off of Mitch. They giggle again and again.

I look in the rearview mirror and I see those sweet faces of my boys, putting a smile on my face. They are safe; we all are.

"Shhhhhhhhh... Mom!" Connor points at my eyes in the mirror, forcing whatever conversation in the back seat to stop.

Frowning, I say, "Shhh?"

Connor grins, "Yes, Mom, it's a surprise!"

We now pull out of the community and head to the main highway. "What's my surprise?" I say with curiosity as I'm looking at the traffic light and then glancing back in my rearview mirror.

Connor says, "Forever, Mommy. Forever. He will love you forever!"

Something grabs my attention in the very back row of seats behind Connor and Logan.

The color red bobs and bobs, and all the air escapes my body; it feels like I'm having an out-of-body experience when I realize what it is I'm watching. It's the balloon; the ruby red balloon left back at the house high up on the window sill. The balloon is bobbing in the back as if someone is yanking on the string. Bob after bob, up and down. It was just bouncing and bouncing. The familiar and terrifying giggle erupts from the very back seat.

"He will love you forever, Mom, just like me!"

ACKNOWLEDGMENTS

I want to take a minute and thank so many people for playing such a vital role in writing Vacant.

First, I would like to thank my husband for not only encouraging me to follow a dream on my bucket list, but for living through this surreal event with me. There is no one on the face of the earth that I would rather go through something like this with than you. I'm truly blessed to have you by my side.

Too my two boys, Mommy is so darn grateful for your endless hugs and support during my many days and nights of writing. Everything I do is for the two of you.

To my parents, thanks so much for supporting me in this dream. Being a part of it, living through it with me step by step as it morphed into a completed novel. Your capacity to give such love and support made this possible.

For the rest of my family and friends, thanks for your encouragement. It was a dream I picked up and ran with the support of everyone close to me. Having the blessing of living in so many different places has given me the gift of endless friendships all over the globe. I hold them all near and dear to my heart.

Big thanks to The Paper House for doing such an amazing job with my cover, editing and everything else in between. You made this experience less stressful and more enjoyable for this first-time author. Every single one of you are truly exceptional at what you do. I look forward to working with you all again in the future.

To anyone out there that has a dream, follow it. Do it for yourself, let it complete you.

I'm a mom who had a dream to write a book and as my husband once said to me, "What are you waiting for, chase your dream."

ABOUT THE AUTHOR

S. Graham was born in Kelowna BC, Canada. She is a wife and very proud mother of two children, currently putting down some roots in The Woodlands, Texas. If she isn't writing you can find her with either a paint brush in her hand re doing antique furniture, or reading a good page turner. Vacant is S. Graham's very first book of many more to come.

CPSIA information can be obtained
at www.ICGtesting.com
Printed in the USA
LVHW081305140522
718771LV00006B/82

9 781087 952468